it's in his Christmas Wish

D1044304

SHELLY ALEXANDER

ALSO BY SHELLY ALEXANDER

Shelly's titles with a little less steam (still sexy, though!):

The Red River Valley Series

It's In His Heart – Coop & Ella's Story

It's In His Touch – Blake & Angelique's Story

It's In His Smile – Talmadge & Miranda's Story

It's In His Arms – Mitchell & Lorenda's Story

It's In His Forever - Langston & His Secret Love's Story

It's In His Song - Dylan & Hailey's Story

It's In His Christmas Wish - Ross & Kimberly's Story

The Angel Fire Falls Series

Dare Me Once — Trace & Lily's Story

Dare Me Again — Elliott & Rebel's Story

Dare Me Now - TBA

Dare Me Always - TBA

Shelly's sizzling titles (with a lot of steam):

The Checkmate Inc. Series

ForePlay – Leo & Chloe's Story

Rookie Moves – Dex & Ava's Story

Get Wilde – Ethan & Adeline's Story

Sinful Games – Oz & Kendall's Story

Wilde Rush - Jacob & Grace's Story TBA

A PERSONAL MESSAGE FROM SHELLY:

Hello, my lovelies,

As this — my first published series — comes to a close, I'm both excited to start new books set in a different location and sad that the wonderfully quirky characters who make up the heart of Red River will no longer be my focus when I sit down to write every day.

Thank you for following this series from start to finish. It's been a fantastic journey, and just like the characters in the books, there has been ups and there has been downs. But you all have stayed with me every step of the way, and for that, I am eternally grateful.

So, enjoy Ross and Kimberly's heartwarming holiday story, and savor the journey through Red River, one last time.

DEDICATION

I'd like to dedicate this book to my sister-in-law, Lisa. When Kimberly's character came to life on the page as a secondary in book 2, her personality and looks were yours to a T. As we spend your last days with you, my imagination has given you the happy ending you deserved. We'll see you in Heaven some day when our time comes.

And as always, for my family:
__Blair Sr., Blair Jr., Elliott, and Nicki__.
You never let me give up, no matter what you had to sacrifice so that I could pursue my dream.
I love all of you more than you'll ever know.

CHAPTER ONE

"Wow. Those are some really big balls," Kimberly Perez deadpanned, studying the examples of new, giant Christmas ornaments that would decorate Red River if the town council voted to purchase them.

Ms. Francine—head of the Christmas decorations committee for at least the last forty years—was in the process of lining up the visual aids on easels in front of the long bar at Cotton Eyed Joe's so the town council could study her selections. The proposed holiday décor would trim Main Street, the park, and the gazebo, which sat smack in the middle of Red River.

Squinting behind glasses as thick as a soda bottle, Ms. Francine set up one enlarged picture after another to illustrate the decorations. Her mysterious purse, which she guarded with her life and was the size of a moving truck, dangled from the notch of her elbow.

Now that took talent.

Clickity, click, click. Kimberly drummed a set of bright blue painted nails against the table and waited her turn to speak at the emergency council meeting.

On a cold Friday morning in early December, dozens of residents had braved the bitter weather just to vote on new decorations, and most of those were older church-going folks who wanted to make sure a Nativity scene was included.

Kimberly stopped the nail drumming. A baby with no crib for a bed was something she could understand. The gazillion foster homes she'd lived in while growing up didn't always have comfy beds, either.

She formed a large circle with her arms, as though she was dancing to a Village People song. "Those are mammoth sized balls, actually."

A few of the meeting attendees chuckled. The rest sniffed at her, then looked down their noses.

Sheesh. Some folks had no sense of humor.

"Thank you, Kimberly," Ms. Francine cooed, as though it had been a compliment. On the last easel, she placed a picture of a pyramid as tall as a house and constructed of gigantic red and green ornamental balls. The pyramid matched the decorations on the other pictures—clusters of gigantic round ornaments hanging from light poles and strung around the gazebo. "When I searched the catalogues for commercial decorations, I really liked the big balls theme," she said innocently. "They just jumped out at me."

Kimberly snorted with laughter, which drew more censuring looks.

Since the meeting was taking place at Red River's favorite watering hole, so Chairperson Clydelle and her sister, Ms. Francine, could have endless refills of heavily spiked coffee at their disposal, Kimberly waved over the new owner. "Dylan, the next round of coffee is on me." She tilted her head toward the group, which didn't seem to appreciate her humor, and whispered, "Sneak the hard stuff into theirs. They need to loosen up."

"Anything for you, Kimberly," he said with a wink.

She looked up at him from under shuttered lashes. "Sure you're taken?"

He smiled. "Yup," he said, then headed back to the bar.

She knew he was, which was the only reason she teased him with such innuendo. Several months back, he'd discovered he had a kid he'd never known about with an old flame. They'd managed to work it out and fall in love in the process. The wedding was set for next summer.

A rush of air slipped through Kimberly's lips and her shoulders slumped.

Weddings. Cribs and high chairs. Love that lasted a lifetime.

Experiences Kimberly would never have.

She'd accepted a long time ago that she was broken on the inside and always would be. Growing up in foster care did that to a person.

She filled her lungs with a deep breath and sat straighter.

Self-pity was her enemy.

Instead, she'd devoted her life and her legal career to helping at-risk children and abused women. Didn't pay much, but she slept like a baby at night because her conscience was clear. Unlike it would've been if she'd pulled down six figures a year—four times over—by representing drug dealers, pimps, gangsters, or any number of other shady characters.

No thank you. She'd keep her thrifty wardrobe, pieced together from resale shops, before she'd sell her soul to defend exactly the kind of people who'd turned both of her parents into addicts.

Ms. Francine stepped back to admire her display, and chitter chatter buzzed through the room. Some wanted a traditional green and red color scheme. Others wanted to try something new, like silver and blue.

Kimberly's nails clicked against the scarred table again. It was almost her turn to plead her persuasive case ... her oral argument ... her courtroom summation to convince the town council to put the money to better use than wasting it on unnecessary materialism and frivolous holiday decorations. Using the money to deliver gifts to kids, who otherwise wouldn't get a single present, seemed more like the *true* spirit of Christmas. The town was already a winter wonderland during the holiday season, and most businesses along Main Street decorated their storefronts on their own with lights, garland, and Santa with his elves painted on their shop windows. Couldn't that suffice for the sake of impoverished kids?

"They sure are nice balls," said Chairperson Clydelle. "I'd like to thank my sister, Francine, for coming up with the idea on such short notice. I knew I could trust her to do Red River proud after a family of raccoons and at least one skunk got into the storage unit where our usual decorations were stored. There was nothing left of them." She wrinkled her nose. "I couldn't eat for a week because of the smell."

"You're very welcome." Ms. Francine's eyes and batting lashes were magnified by her thick glasses. "With just three weeks until Christmas, a lot of companies were low on inventory, but they've got plenty of big balls." She touched an index finger to her wrinkled lips. "I've always appreciated a nice set of balls."

Kimberly almost lost it.

So did some of the other attendees, because either muffled laughter or sniffs of disapproval rounded the room.

When Ms. Francine opened a large box and pulled out two huge Christmas ornamental balls strung together with a long, thick icicle hanging between them and put it on display alongside the easels, the entire room went quiet. When she added a clump of holly between the balls, the church contingency gasped in horror. Everyone else nearly fell out of their chairs, unable to hide their laughter.

Good to know some of the locals *could* find humor in life. Her bestie, Angelique Barbetta-Holloway, had all but brow-beaten Kimberly into finally joining their legal minds right there in Red River, swearing it was a win-win. Kimberly would hate to think she'd finally uprooted her practice in Taos, forty-five minutes away, only to discover her misfit ways were too much for small town culture.

One of the council members—an older man wearing a winter duck hunting hat with flaps covering his ears—stood. "As the council treasurer, I'll go over the costs and the budget we'll need to purchase the new decorations." He started spitting out numbers quicker than a lottery ticket dispenser.

The front door of Joe's swung open and in walked Ross Armstrong. He was a hulking guy with thick, sandy blond hair, and just enough scruff on his jaw to give him a tough but lovable look. His usual ball cap, which he always wore backward, was replaced with a black knit beanie to accommodate the winter weather. His standard insulated coveralls weren't greased up yet, since he likely stopped at the early morning meeting before opening his mechanic shop for the day.

Kimberly's insides sighed.

His last name fit him as nicely as his coveralls, and that was saying something. Not many men could make coveralls look sexy as hell.

They'd been pals ever since she first started hanging out in Red River with Angelique a few years before, and Ross had led her around the dance floor at Joe's in a country and western two-step many, many times.

So she knew how strong his arms really were. Yes indeedy.

When he glanced around the room, and his gaze landed on her, the sigh whispering through her body turned to a hum. When he headed in her direction with a friendly smile on his face, the hum turned to an electric buzz.

Without thinking, she smoothed a hand over her cropped hair, caught herself, then dropped her hand to her lap.

You look exactly the way you should, dummy.

The platinum-white hair she created with a do-it-yourself dye kit and the outlandish clothes had started years ago when she was a rebellious teenager bouncing around the foster system. Vices that were less harmful than, say, drugs.

When she was working three jobs and relying on financial aid to put herself through undergrad and law school, she'd realized the unusual choice of hair and clothing could also serve as a repellent to keep away the *right* kind of men. So she'd kept that style—if one could call it that—going, making it her trademark.

Ross kept ambling in her direction, his smooth confident gait commanding the room.

Of course, it could've been that his presence had that effect only on her.

His eyes stayed firmly planted on her, and that sexy half-cocked smile of his made her want to lick her lips. His hair, still slightly damp, curled around the bottom of his knit cap, and made her wish she'd been the one lathering it up under a hot shower.

Gack!

Maybe she should've shaved off all of her hair instead of just dying it. Maybe tattooing her entire face would've been more repulsive than her outrageous wardrobe. Now, *that* would've been an epic nice-guy repellant.

He stopped to say hello to a table of council attendees two rows away, and she relaxed.

After a few words, he strode in her direction again.

No, no, *no.*

She propped her feet in the empty chair next to her, crossing her purple sequined Uggs at the ankles.

"Nice boots." Ross stared at her feet.

"Thank you." She gave him a brief glance, then trained her eyes on the ornament samples at the front of the room. "I got them for cents on the dollar at a thrift shop." No idea why she said that.

"That's nice." He pushed her feet off the chair. "Now move 'em," he said in that friendly banter they always used with one another. He slid into the seat, angling his body toward her, as though they were intimately acquainted.

She could do this. They were friends.

Never mind that Ladyland had started going rogue several months back every time she saw him. She'd stopped dancing with him. Started avoiding him. And definitely did not continue the harmless flirting that used to make them both laugh over a beer at Joe's.

Because it wasn't exactly harmless anymore. Somewhere along

the line, she'd realized she cared about him. As in really, *really* cared about him.

And she wouldn't wish herself on her worst enemy, much less someone she cared about.

Involuntarily, she breathed in his masculine soap and fresh shampoo that reminded her of soft rain on a warm summer day.

Her skin prickled.

He leaned close and whispered, "Or you can set your feet in my lap."

A shiver skated over her.

She swallowed and pulled herself together. "No thanks."

She focused on Councilman Flaps, who had moved on from the cost of the actual decorations to postage and delivery fees.

"Hey." Ross kept his voice low so only she could hear. "Haven't seen you around in a while. If I didn't know better, I'd think you've been avoiding me."

"Hey, big guy." She slugged his arm in the same friendly way that had been her usual greeting. He'd never ever have to know that she'd rather roll up his sleeve and trace the tattoo on his arm with her tongue. "I've been around. Just busy."

Chairperson Clydelle opened the floor for a discussion, at which point an argument broke out because Jesus wasn't represented in the proposed décor. The church folks wanted it. Ms. Francine and her supporters didn't, opting for the pyramid of giant balls to go in the park instead of a Nativity scene. The church folks said something about a lot of souls burning in hell.

Kimberly couldn't resist a pun that easy. "Holy smokes."

Ross belted out a deep rumbling laugh.

Which made a kaleidoscope of butterflies take flight in her stomach.

"Good one." Ross returned her fake slug with a gentle tap to her arm.

And the butterflies swarmed and swirled faster.

One of the church elders pulled a pocket-sized Bible from his jacket, turned to a pre-marked page, and quoted scriptures about the fires of hell, which the council would all experience if Jesus was removed from Red River's Christmas décor theme. At which point, Ms. Francine—with the politest tone—told them they could go to hell themselves.

Kimberly rolled her eyes heavenward.

She wasn't a super religious person, but she did know enough to understand that Jesus probably didn't care about superficial decorations any more than she did. It was the heart behind it all that mattered, especially during a holiday that was supposed to represent giving instead of receiving. Unity and peace instead of threats and division.

So, she'd let them fight it out amongst themselves, priming the pump for her suggestion to use the money to help underprivileged kids instead. Court room arguments had taught her that going last was the best strategy, because it left the most impact on the judge or jury.

She tried to make small talk with Ross, thankful her bouncing leg was hidden under the table. "What brings you to a town council meeting on this fine colder-than-a-witch's-tata day?"

Kimberly knew she was a lot of things. Smart. Studious. Self-sufficient.

Tact was at the bottom of her list of endearing traits, right along with her fashion sense, and both could work in her favor when she wanted to chase away someone.

Ross made a motion to Dylan, who was behind the bar. Dylan nodded, obviously knowing what Ross wanted without him actually having to place a verbal order.

Ross shook his head in disgust. "I heard someone in town has gone full-on Grinch, and I came to stop them."

"*Who?*" The irony of Whoville in that age-old Christmas tale wasn't lost on either of them, and they both snorted at the same time.

Jeez, she cracked herself up.

"Seriously, who?" She had no idea what he was talking about.

He shrugged. "No idea. That's what I'm here to find out, so

they don't ruin Christmas for the rest of us. I mean, what kind of person wouldn't want Red River to be decked out for the holidays?"

Obviously, she wasn't in the loop regarding the latest Red River drama because she wasn't aware of anyone who wanted to ruin Christmas for the entire town.

Oh. Wait...

Her leg bounced so fast, and furiously, the table shook, but it didn't compare to the quake of nerves rocking her insides.

She looked down at her fingers, and could swear her skin was taking on a greenish hue. She angled her head to one side and studied her hands. Was that green fur sprouting on her knuckles and around her fingertips?

Joe's suddenly seemed very, very warm.

She'd kept the idea she'd planned to pitch to the town council on the down-low so the element of surprise would work in her favor. How in the world had her secret gotten out?

And I'm just now hearing that in my head. This was Red River, where few secrets could be kept.

"Sounds like gossip to me." She waved a hand in the air. "I'm sure it's been twisted into something very different than what it was meant to be."

"Chairperson Clydelle and Ms. Francine alerted me that there might be a troublemaker at the meeting who had a problem with buying new decorations," Ross said.

Ah. Kimberly all but sniffed the air for two rats who wore thick glasses and had silver hair. It was no secret that Kimberly was thrifty.

Okay, she was a complete tightwad, so when she'd asked to be included on the agenda, Chairperson Clydelle and Ms. Francine must've gotten suspicious as to her reasons.

Dylan walked over and put a piping hot cup of coffee in front of Ross. "Your usual."

The two men fist bumped. "That's why Joe's is the busiest foodie establishment in town."

When Dylan was gone, Ross went back to grousing about the unidentified green monster.

"Why is this so important to you?" Kimberly half-scoffed. "I've seen your shop and the lodge you own next to it. You string enough lights on your businesses to shut down the power grids throughout the entire Rockies." She laughed and gave his shoulder a friendly push.

Her laugher sputtered to a stop when he didn't respond.

Instead, he circled the rim of his coffee mug with a fingertip and stared down into the dark liquid, as though it was a mirror into his soul. "Christmas is special ... because..."

Councilman Flaps finished his accounting report and sat down.

Ross let a sad sigh slip through his lips. "It doesn't matter why it's important to me. It just is, and I don't know who came up with such a ridiculous idea, but I can't let anyone steal Christmas from Red River." Ross sipped his coffee, steam swirling into his bad-boy 'stache.

"Um, well." Maybe her idea to speak last wasn't the brightest in this case. *Maybe* presenting her idea should've been first on the agenda before Ross walked in and threw her off her game. Or realized she was the She-Grinch in question, even though he was mistaken when it came to her intent. She didn't want to ruin Christmas. Contrary to what he'd obviously been led to believe, she wanted to make the holiday extraordinary for kids who rarely, if ever, got a Christmas at all. "I wouldn't necessarily call it stealing Christmas."

Ross kept gazing into his mug, as though it was a crystal ball. Sorrow filled his eyes, and his usual easy-going countenance drained away, replaced by a heaviness that rolled off him in waves.

"Ross, what is it?" she whispered, placing a hand on his arm.

He snapped out of his trance and blew on the steaming liquid, then took a sip. The muscle in his squared jaw hardened. "If this Grinch person doesn't want to celebrate Christmas..."

"There are a lot of different ways to celebrate the holidays." She pulled her hand away from his arm and instantly missed the contact. "A few less decorations won't stop anyone from celebrating."

He rolled right over her comments. "They don't have to celebrate it, but for some of us, Christmas is a tradition." His strong jaw released and tensed again. "It represents loved ones and memories that shouldn't be forgotten, so why cancel it for everyone?"

"I wouldn't really call it canceling Christmas, either," she said with the same meekness she'd felt every time she'd had to walk into a new foster home for the first time.

Sure, she got it that the holidays meant something to most families in a way that was elusive to her because of her upbringing. The holidays also represented commercialism, and seemed like an excuse to spend gobs of money on things that people didn't really need.

"I think you're blowing this out of proportion, Ross."

Ross's gaze slid away from his mug and locked with hers. "What are you saying, Kimberly?" He didn't let her answer. "Do you think the Grinch is right?"

When the table began to rock back and forth from her bouncing leg, she slipped a hand under the table, placed it on her thigh—which was clad in red and green reindeer leggings, so where did he get off calling her a Grinch, anyway—and dug a set of nails into her own flesh to still her limb.

"*Owwsh,*" she hissed under her breath.

Ross let his mug hover at his lips. "You okay?" His tone softened with concern.

"Yep." She pushed back, scooting her chair out from under the table. "I just remembered I had something important on my schedule this morning."

Like finding a hole to crawl into until the holidays were over. Or climbing to the top of Wheeler Peak, which loomed over Red River, to see if she could find a cave, a sled, and a little dog to slap fake antlers onto.

As she started to stand, Chairperson Clydelle pounded a gavel, as though she was a Supreme Court judge, and read from a sheet of paper in front of her. "Kimberly Perez."

Kimberly halted her attempt to straighten and froze in a weird half crouch, half standing position.

Chairperson Clydelle looked up from her paper. "You've asked to be put on the agenda to speak before we vote on the new decorations. You've got complaints over expanding the budget, I presume?"

Kimberly narrowed her eyes at Chairperson Clydelle and Ms. Francine. Superpowers when it came to reading people must run in their bloodline, because yep. Those two old widowed sisters had definitely figured out why Kimberly had come to the meeting, and they'd called in help from the hottest mechanic in town. It couldn't be a coincidence that the mechanic also happened to be Kimberly's dancing and drinking buddy until recently. And was hotter than a five alarm fire.

Well, the joke was on them, because Kimberly had put a stop to buddying around with Ross.

Chairperson Clydelle and Ms. Francine leveled laser stares at her, waiting for her to respond.

Obviously, they knew Kimberly hated wasteful spending. They just didn't know why she despised it so much. Kimberly didn't talk about her upbringing with anyone but her bestie, Angelique.

Superpowers aside, the fact that Kimberly had shown up at last summer's council meeting armed with financial pie charts before they'd voted on renovating the Chamber of Commerce building had probably tipped them off as to why she wanted to speak at today's meeting. She'd won that battle, convincing the council to sow those precious funds into local kids by building a new playground in the park instead.

Now, the kids filtering through her office had a place to play while their mothers, or guardians, or case workers came from far and wide to utilize the pro bono work Kimberly offered.

Winning this battle wasn't going to be so easy because those two shrewd silver-haired sisters had come prepared with an ambush.

Kimberly's gaze darted to Ross.

His expression was still stern. Not something she was used to from him, and he watched her expectantly. He was obviously still unaware that she was the one who had a heart three sizes too small.

It was now or never. And since she didn't plan on following through on her feelings for him because she was too much of a black sheep to make anybody happy, she said, "I'm sorry, Ross."

She turned her attention to the council members. "I'd like to propose a new city ordinance that cuts all holiday decorations and costly festivities from the city budget." Damn, she really could use that spiked coffee right about now. A little liquid courage never hurt. "I'd also like to propose we find alternative ways to celebrate that don't cost anything, so the money can be an annual contribution to kids in our area who won't receive a gift from any other source."

From the corner of her eye, she saw Ross go deathly still. Except for his coffee mug, which tipped to the right just enough to slosh coffee onto his coveralls. He didn't move. Didn't wipe off the coffee. He just kept staring at her, as though she was ... well, the Red River Grinch.

CHAPTER TWO

"*You?*" Ross rasped out over the rim of his steaming hot coffee mug. "But why, Kimberly?"

He'd thought he was going to the meeting to stop a horrible person from ruining Christmas. From depriving him of what his sister had asked of him, once Noelle's doctors informed their family it would be her last holiday season.

Always celebrate Christmas to the fullest.

He'd followed through on his promise every year since. He wasn't about to stop now.

Kimberly was the Grinch?

He was trying really, really hard to wrap his head around that surprise development.

She was one of the best people he'd ever met. Definitely the most interesting, with her larger-than-life personality and peculiar appearance. When everyone else raised a brow over her free-spirit ways and blunt talk, he found himself chuckling because a warmth flowed through his veins and filled his chest. He loved her boldness. It was refreshing and attractive.

It hadn't occurred to him that she'd turn out to be the Red River Grinch.

"I, well..." Kimberly stammered, then leaned over to talk specifically to him. "I'm explaining why. This isn't personal, Ross."

Sure as hell felt personal.

Celebrating Christmas with decking the halls, trimming the trees, *fa la la la la-ing*, and anything and everything else that went along with the holidays was how he kept his sister's memory alive. Noelle was born on Christmas day, so naturally, it had been her favorite holiday, with their family going all out to celebrate both occasions every year.

Until she'd passed away the week between Christmas and New Year's, when she was twelve and Ross had been just sixteen. After that, his parents had stopped celebrating all together, so it was up to Ross to honor her last wish.

As Kimberly continued her speech about the wastefulness of decorations, Ross retrieved his phone from his pocket and sent an SOS message to every Red River resident in his contacts list. Time to bring in reinforcements to save Christmas.

And to save Kimberly from herself. Hating on holiday decorations wasn't the Kimberly he knew. The Kimberly he'd secretly come to care for. The Kimberly he'd been waiting patiently to open her heart to him and give him a chance at being more than just a friend.

Hadn't happened.

He'd waited a long time for the right woman to come along. Even her wild hair and clothes hadn't scared him off, which she wore like armor. It was obvious that she didn't let most people get too close, and when something beyond friendship had stirred between her and Ross several months ago, she'd all but severed contact.

Kimberly went on about how underprivileged kids would benefit if Red River didn't buy new decorations.

Her heart was in the right place, he'd give her that. Ross donated plenty to charity, too, but why take away the cheerful decorations and bright twinkling lights, which every kid on the planet loved?

The front door of Joe's opened and dozens more people started filtering in, all from Ross's contacts list.

One of the perks of living in a small town—Red River was a tight-knit community. Sort of like a family who argued with each other but had each other's backs, too. One text calling for help with very little explanation, except that their presence was needed to stop Christmas in Red River from being ruined, was all it took for most of the town to show up and offer support. By the time they finished filing in, it was standing room only in Joe's.

Kimberly faltered. Went quiet.

She seemed to straighten her spine and square her shoulders. Only the quiver of her plump bottom lip gave away how nervous she really was underneath the adversarial attorney routine.

That quivering lip chipped away at Ross's resolve, and he seriously considered giving her what she wanted. He took out his wallet and stared at Noelle's picture in a Santa hat and jingle bell earrings. It had been taken a few weeks before she passed.

That's all it took for his resolve to turn to steel again, and he shoved his wallet back into his pocket.

Kimberly walked to the front and picked up one of the big balls that Ms. Francine had pulled from a box to put on display as an example. "Do we really want to spend our money on this, when the money could make a difference in so many children's lives?" She gave the ball a boost.

The shiny material must've been more slippery than she'd thought because it popped from her grasp.

Her expression turned bewildered, as though she couldn't believe what was happening.

The giant ornament crashed to the ground, shattering in a million pieces.

Someone from Ross's SOS responders yelled out, "You did that on purpose!"

Both of Kimberly's hands flew to her mouth. "I didn't mean—"

"Grinch!" another of Ross's contacts shouted.

Oh, shit. He'd called them in as an SOS support team, not a hit squad.

He might disagree with Kimberly not wanting to purchase new decorations for Red River, but she wouldn't have broken the ornament on purpose.

He stood. "I don't think she—"

Chairperson Clydelle banged her gavel. "I agree with Mr. Armstrong. I don't think Ms. Perez understands the implications of what she's proposing. Red River without holiday decorations just wouldn't be Red River at all. It might even hurt our holiday tourism."

What? That wasn't at all what he was going to say, and he was beginning to suspect he'd been had by the chairperson and her sidekick sister.

Kimberly's expression turned from disbelief over the shattered ornament, to confusion as she looked up at Chairperson Clydelle. Then her look darkened to disappointment, finally morphing into betrayal when her gaze locked onto Ross.

"If the decorations are that fragile, then they aren't worth what they cost. They won't last the winter with the kind of wind and snowstorms we get in Red River." Kimberly folded both arms. "The money really could be better spent, and these decorations would be a careless and irresponsible way to use our town's funds."

The churchgoers mumbled and nodded their approval. Their ring leader held his small Bible in the air. "I agree with Ms. Perez. If Jesus isn't going to be represented in the decorations, then we ought not have decorations at all."

"Well." Kimberly paled. "That's not exactly what I meant—"

"We want Christmas decorations!" someone shouted from Team SOS.

An argument between the two sides broke out, with most everyone yelling.

Deep red crept up Kimberly's neck and into her face.

He'd like to say the color change to her skin made her hazel eyes turn Grinch-green, but that would be a lie. They deepened to gorgeous glittering emerald.

Ross reminded himself to stay strong. No matter how sensual he found the rapidly beating pulse at the base of her neck, no matter how good her intentions were, she was his rival on this issue. Not his friend. And not his lover.

Unfortunately.

Still, he could not, under any circumstances, let her take Christmas away from Red River. "We could find more durable decorations." His comment wasn't heard over the din of arguing.

Chairperson Clydelle thumped her gavel against the table until the crowd quieted. "Now that we've heard from everyone, are we ready to put the big balls to a vote?"

Normally, that was exactly the type of comment that would have Kimberly snorting with laughter while using her razor-sharp wit to spit out a pun faster than anyone else he knew. Ross would usually laugh along with her, because watching her snort was hilarious and warmed his insides like nothing he'd ever experienced. But seeing his sister's last wishes carried out was too serious, so instead of laughing at Ms. Francine's unfortunate description of the holiday decorations, he raised an index finger. "I have something to say."

Chairperson Clydelle sighed, but one side of her wrinkled lips twitched, as though she was fighting off a smile of victory. "Go ahead."

"Look around." He swept a hand across the room. "One text from me, and all of these people showed up because they want to celebrate Christmas the way we always have in Red River."

"You called on most of the town residents to shoot down my idea to help little kids?" Kimberly let her jaw hang open dramatically. "Wow, Ross. I didn't realize I was such a threat."

Okay, texting his entire contacts list may have been an overreaction. He'd been so disappointed when he'd found out who wanted to ban Christmas in Red River, that he'd overcompensated.

"Why can't we find a middle ground and do both? We could help children *and* decorate Red River at the same time."

"We can help even more kids if you don't spend *any* money on decorations," Kimberly huffed.

The room erupted into arguing again, with both sides squaring off against each other.

Chairperson Clydelle steepled her fingers and watched the show.

Kimberly kept her arms folded and tapped a foot. The look on her face said steam might as well billow from her ears.

Ross thumped a thumb against the table.

An advocate for a Nativity scene stood. "We'll boycott every business in town whose owners want the decorations!"

"That's your way of spreading good will?" grumbled one of the guys who'd shown up because of Ross's text. "In return, we'll call every newspaper and television station in the state and have them film us protesting your picket lines because you're trying to cancel Jesus's birthday."

"This is getting out of hand." Kimberly threw up her hands. "But if you can't listen to reason, then you're leaving me no choice but to fight for what *I* believe in, and that's the welfare of children. Not meaningless decorations."

"Meaningless?" Ross crossed his arms, too, digging in for a fight. "If it's a fued you want, then you've got it."

"Have a seat, Ms. Perez," Chairperson Clydelle commanded.

The battle between opposing sides—decorations or no decorations—erupted again, raging around him as Kimberly skulked back to her chair. When she sat, she scooted several inches away from him.

Ross eased closer. "Kimberly, why are you doing this? I'll go to war with every person in this town to protect Christmas."

He'd go to war with every person in the world if it meant honoring his sister's last wishes. Her love of Christmas was all he had left of her.

Grief welled up and caught in his throat.

When his parents abandoned Christmas all together because of the painful reminder, he'd felt her death all over again. They'd refused to speak of her, as though she'd never existed. So, once Ross was grown and could do as he pleased, he'd celebrated the holidays every year, the way she'd asked him to do.

It was the only way he could deal with Christmas without agonizing heartbreak engulfing him.

It had caused a riff so deep and wide between him and his folks, they'd finally sold *Papa Bear's Lodge* to him and moved outside of Red River. Living farther out of town, they didn't have to see Red River lit up every Christmas, and Ross could carry on Noelle's wishes without feeling guilty about what it did to his mom and dad.

Time hadn't helped them heal, so Ross visited them less and less. He resented not being able to speak Noelle's name in their presence, or reminisce over her memories in their home.

What kind of people did that?

Yet he loved his parents dearly, and the last thing he wanted was to cause them more pain. So he stayed away to protect himself and them, too.

Finally, Chairperson Clydelle banged her gavel and held up a hand. "Enough. I've heard all I need to." She turned her gaze on Kimberly and pointed the gavel at her. "You."

Kimberly's eyes flew wide.

Satisfaction rose in Ross's chest to snuff out some of the grief. *Christmas decorations—1, Grinch—0.* As much as he cared for Kimberly, she was flat wrong. There was no reason they couldn't accomplish both of their goals at the same time, so he let his lips curve into a smile.

Until Chairperson Clydelle's gavel swung in his direction. "And you."

He let the smile fall from his lips and looked around, hoping she was pointing at someone else.

"Yes, *you,* Mr. Armstrong." Then Chairperson Clydelle put

Kimberly back in her crosshairs. "Since the two of you have managed to divide the entire town during a season when we're supposed to come together as a community, I'm going to move that we postpone the vote on the new decorations and on the city ordinance."

"I second the motion," said Councilman Flaps.

"All in favor?" Chairperson Clydelle didn't bother to wait for a response. She pounded the gavel again. "Motion passed."

"But what about the big balls?" Ms. Francine all but whined.

Chairperson Clydelle harrumphed. "If the council votes for them, it'll look like we don't care about the kids. If the council votes against them, we'll look like a bunch of Scrooges."

Ross pointed at Kimberly. "She's already got the bah-humbug market cornered."

Kimberly gave him a scalding glare. "*Me?*" Her tone hardened. "You're the one who doesn't want to help the Tiny Tims of our community." She pursed her lips. "Seems to me that I'm not the only person in the room named Ebenezer. Besides," she gave him a haughty look, "you're getting your Christmas stories mixed up. You started the meeting by referring to me as the Grinch."

He leaned in so only she could hear an gave her a sly smile. "Not your usual witty comeback, Kimberly. You must be desperate." He let his smile widen. "Or maybe a little shaken."

"Ha! I'm rock solid." She gave him a look of contempt, but her chin still quivered, telling him she was as shaken as a damn snow globe in a souvenir shop.

"Seems to me Ms. Perez is both Grinch and Scrooge," one of Ross's supporters said.

"Order!" Chairperson Clydelle hammered on the table again. "Red River was already running behind on our holiday schedule because of the raccoon and skunk fiasco, but now our little town is blowing apart at the seams because of the cost of harmless decorations. So, the two of you can darn well fix this." Chairperson Clydelle's scolding gaze bounced from Ross to Kimberly, as though they were children.

Ross seriously felt as though he might be sent to his room without dinner.

Kimberly shot a look at him, then her eyes darted away. "Um, how? I mean, I didn't want to cause trouble. I only meant for us to bring a little joy to children's lives."

Chairperson Clydelle waved her gavel around the scowling room. "Well, you can see for yourself how successful you were at the *bringing joy* part of your plan. Thanks for that, by the way. Dealing with this kind of mess is every chairperson's nightmare during the holidays," she deadpanned.

Kimberly tugged at an earlobe, which had a line of studs pierced into it all the way around the rim. "Sorry, I—"

"Enough talk from you," Chairperson Clydelle said, then turned her frown back on Ross.

His head snapped back because she and her gavel were kind of frightening.

"Ross Armstrong and Kimberly Perez are responsible for this year's decorations," said Chairperson Clydelle.

"What?" Ross sat up straight.

"Wait!" Kimberly said at the same time.

"*All* the decorations?" Ross blurted.

"For the entire town?" Kimberly shot to her feet.

That ignited another free for all between the townsfolk.

Chairperson Clydelle downed the rest of her spiked coffee, sat her large mug aside, and—in spite of the creamer mustache left on her upper lip—she brought the crowd to heel with three menacing swings of her gavel. "Why don't the two of you start with a Wishing Tree? Setting up a Christmas tree in the park is an important part of our ritual in Red River, and it'll give our town the opportunity to grant a wish to the kids in our community who need them."

"What about the rest of the decorations?" One tree didn't seem sufficient for an entire town, and his sister's memory would seem to fade without twinkling lights and sparkling ornaments everywhere.

Chairperson Clydelle leaned forward on one elbow and waved the gavel at him. "It's your turn to look around, Mr. Armstrong."

He did, and with half of the meeting attendees scowling back at him, he wanted to pull at the neck of his coveralls.

"Now you'll see how it feels for the town council to have to try and make everyone happy. You and Ms. Perez just earned yourselves that responsibility, so go figure it out. I, for one, am going to enjoy watching you try with most of the town breathing down your necks. Since we've had to postpone the vote to expand the budget, you'll have very little funds to work with. Have fun finding a way to put those modest and hard-earned taxpayer dollars to work so both sides get what they want."

Oh. Hell. He'd come to the town council meeting to save Christmas, not to be put in charge of the holidays for the entire town.

"You'll report your progress to me every day, seeing as how Christmas is right around the corner and there's no time to lose." She banged her gavel. "Meeting adjourned."

"But I've got a law practice to run—" Kimberly started to protest, but Chairperson Clydelle mowed her down with an admonishing look.

Kimberly's mouth clamped shut.

"Well, crap on a cracker," Ms. Francine spoke up, her purse still dangling on her arm. "I really wanted those big balls."

Ross had to admit, he'd really like a bigger set of balls, too. He must've left his at home because he felt as though he'd just been manhandled by a petite woman with wild hair and an old lady with a loaded gavel.

CHAPTER THREE

Well, that didn't go as planned.

Even though she was stunned, Kimberly beelined it to the front door before the sound of Chairperson Clydelle's last swing of the gavel finished echoing through Cotton Eyed Joe's.

Kimberly stepped through the door and let it swing shut behind her. Icy winter air slapped her in the face, knocking her back to reality and the problem she'd just created for herself.

Making sure impoverished kids received gifts had been her plan. Somehow, she'd gotten stuck with the responsibility of decorating an entire town for Christmas on a shoestring budget, *and* labeled as the town Grinch.

With a shiver, she stepped onto the snow-packed sidewalk, stopping to pull on a pair of lavender knit gloves with the fingertips cut out and a lime green knit cap.

She'd darn sure decorate on her own, though, because she was not working side by side with Ross Armstrong.

Now, she just had to figure out how to pull off the impossible.

She folded her arms. Tapped her foot. Chewed her lip. Racked her brain on how to fix the hot mess that had just been handed to her.

Her best buddy since law school and legal partner might be

able to help. Together, Angelique and Kimberly had tackled some pretty tough stuff over the years. This should be a piece of fruitcake.

She snorted at the Christmas pun.

Because hell. It was either laugh or cry.

A few people who'd attended the council meeting started to trickle out of Joe's, and she kept her back to the door so she wouldn't have to see their scowling faces.

Sheesh. The way the mob had squared off against each other ... against either her or Ross ... they might as well have been discussing the outcome of, say, a presidential election instead of Christmas décor.

She turned on a heel to head toward her law office, where she and her BFF could put their intelligent heads together.

Strong fingers curled around Kimberly's arm, pulling her to a stop again. "Whoa there," Ross said. "If we're going to work together on decorations, we best get started. We're already in the first week of December."

The stream of meeting attendees filing out of Joe's thickened, all of them glaring at either her or Ross.

"I'm not working with someone who called me both Grinch and Scrooge in the span of sixty seconds," she whispered.

He glanced down at her feet. "If the bedazzled boot fits."

Through gritted teeth, she whispered, "I didn't expect *you* to try and sabotage my dream to help kids who can't help themselves."

He leaned close enough that their noses almost touched. "And I didn't expect *you* to try and sabotage a tradition in this town that everyone loves, *especially* kids."

She glared at him.

He acted as though it didn't bother him in the least. "Now, we have no choice but to work together to make both happen." He looked down at her boots. "If we can't find enough decorations for the whole town, we can string your boots from the street lamps. I have no doubt you've got more." His grin went full-on, lighting his face in that friendly, flirtatious way he had with her.

Ladyland purred.

Down, girl.

She turned a foot on its side and studied her boots. "They're sequined, and they aren't that noticeable. At least not noticeable enough to call them bedazzled."

"I've seen blinking neon signs in Vegas that are less noticeable." He winked, his green eyes sparkling as brightly as her boots. "But I like 'em. They suit you. Now, can we get out of the cold and discuss how to go about decorating a whole town?"

"I can handle it." She stuffed her hands into her pockets. "Leave it to me." She took a step back.

Sarcasm practically dripped from his chuckle. "I'm *not* leaving Christmas to the person who just tried to have it canceled." He stared down at her, that twinkle still flickering in his eyes. "So, your place or mine?"

Ladyland roared.

Bad, girl. Very bad.

"Um, I have a lot of work waiting for me at the office." She shifted from one foot to the other.

A middle-aged couple, who'd shown up late for the council meeting, walked out of Joe's, stopped on the top step, and gave her a stare so cold she could've sworn the icicles hanging from the eaves instantly doubled in size.

Kimberly widened her eyes at the couple and lifted both palms in a *what are you staring at* gesture. "I was trying to help kids. How is that a bad thing?"

The couple walked away, but not without one of them mumbling, "Christmas hating Grinch," under their breath.

Kimberly's mouth fell open, and she let out an exasperated huff. She turned narrowed eyes on Ross and pointed at the retreating couple. "You do realize that's your doing, right?"

He shrugged. "Seemed more like your own doing to me." Then he smiled. "But I have to admit, I did help it along a little."

She rolled her eyes. "I have to live in this town, too, ya know."

"All the more reason we need to kick it into gear," Ross said. "So, when can we meet? I'll make it easy for you and come to your office."

Kimberly folded her arms over the front of her puffy burgundy down jacket and studied him. Ross was such a handsome guy. Not in a *GQ* kind of way. He had more of a rugged mountain man vibe. His hair, which curled up over the edge of his knit cap, was still slightly damp.

Her mouth turned to cotton.

The image of Ross in nothing but a towel draped low around his hips and droplets of water still fresh on his tanned skin was something she shouldn't let herself think on for too long. It made Ladyland scratch and claw for attention.

That just wasn't happening. She liked Ross too much to let him get to know the real Kimberly Perez. The Kimberly who didn't have much to offer, which was why she poured her heart into children who had hard lives just like she'd had. It was the most positive and meaningful thing she had to give.

It was the *only* positive and meaningful thing she had to give.

When Ross leveled a determined stare right back at her and folded his arms over his insulated coveralls, mimicking her stance, she realized how much time had gone by with her staring at him.

She dropped her arms and stood tall.

"Fine. I should be finished with work around five o'clock." Without a good-bye, she stepped off the curb, looked both ways, and started to cross the street to walk to her office in Red River's downtown historic district.

"Good," he called after her. "I'll bring dinner, so don't eat."

When she got to her office, she traipsed up the salted stairs and stomped her feet on the mat in front of the door. As she reached for the doorknob, she chuckled at the new lettering on the door. *Barbetta-Holloway & Perez.* After surviving breast cancer at a young age, Angelique Barbetta had resolved never to marry because she'd felt disfigured. When she fell madly in love with Red

River's handsome country doctor—who Kimberly had nicknamed Dr. Tall, Dark, and Hotsome—and they tied the knot, Angelique had still refused to give up her maiden name and hyphenated it just to tease her wonderful husband.

Kimberly pushed through the door and started pulling off her winter coat to leave in the foyer. "Ang? Are you here?"

"Yep," came a response from Angelique's office.

Kimberly's Uggs squeaked as she walked into Angelique's office and plopped into a chair in front of the desk. "Now that you've added my name to the firm, you do realize I can never get married, right?" Not that she planned to, but she loved to goad her friend about the hyphenated name.

Angelique turned away from her computer and braced her elbows against the desk. "What? Why?"

"Because I'd have to hyphenate my name, too, and it would look ridiculous on the door." Kimberly slumped down in the chair and stared at the ceiling. "And don't get me started on the letterhead and business cards. All those names would never fit."

Angelique glanced at her Apple watch. "Is that what has you in a prickly mood so early in the morning?" She pulled off her glasses, her dark Italian eyes narrowing. "You're worried about how our names will look when you marry..." She tapped her chin, as though she was puzzled. "Who is it you're planning to marry, by the way?"

"No one!" Kimberly let both of her arms hang limp over the sides of the chair.

"Exactly." Angelique slid the glasses back onto her nose and went back to typing. "So, what's with all the theatrics at this early hour?"

"I bombed at the council meeting." Kimberly threw an arm over her face.

Angelique stopped typing, dipped her chin, and looked over the rim of her tortoise glasses. "You're an awesome communicator. The best I've ever seen at negotiating disputes and delivering closing arguments. It couldn't have been that bad."

Normally, that would be true. Until a certain mechanic had

walked in and labeled her as the Red River Grinch. "Girlfriend, I bombed so badly that I took out half of North America."

"What in the world happened at that meeting?" Angelique asked.

Kimberly relayed the whole story.

When she was done, Angelique said, "Damn. Those two elderly sisters were scary enough with their purse and cane. Who the heck gave Ms. Clydelle a gavel?"

"No idea." Kimberly shook her head. "But I swear, I think it was monogramed with her initials, and she's obviously not afraid to use it. Maybe I should go confront her one on one and tell her that I simply refuse to do what she says. I could dig my heels in and do the Wishing Tree, but none of the other decorations, since the tree accomplishes my goal to begin with." The thought of standing up to Ms. Clydelle was actually kind of unnerving, even for a tough girl like Kimberly who'd had to fend for herself most of her life.

Angelique's silky black brow arched. "Brave but foolish. Going against Ms. Clydelle would likely set off another explosion big enough to take out the other half of North America, and possibly Central and South America, too."

"True. Canada and Peru are on my must-see list, so they're probably worth saving. The problem is..." Accomplishing a big project like decorating an entire town without throwing herself into Ross's arms and kissing him silly might be harder than Kimberly cared to admit.

But she couldn't. She *wouldn't*.

If she let him see beneath the flamboyant exterior, he'd know the truth. She wasn't a whole person on the inside. A fact she'd rather keep to herself. For the rest of her life, thank you very much.

Angelique rolled an index finger in a *keep talking* gesture. "What's the problem?"

Kimberly shook her head because Angelique would tell her that she was being foolish to keep her distance from Ross. Her buddy, who knew her better than anyone, still wouldn't understand, because Angelique had grown up with a close, loving family and didn't have the hang-ups of a foster kid. "Nothing. Never mind."

"So, what are you going to do?" Angelique asked.

"Well, first, I'm going to go flog myself for opening my big fat mouth." Kimberly scooted to the edge of her chair and ran a set of fingers through her short blonde hair. "Forty or so lashes should do it."

Angelique nodded. "Melodramatic, but okay. Whatever works for you, girlfriend."

Kimberly pushed out of her chair with a deep exhale. "After that, I guess I'll get my ass moving and get the job done. Ross will be here after work. He was a victim of Chairperson Clydelle's gavel, too, and has to work with me on the decorations." Kimberly scrunched her shoulders and held her thumb and forefinger a half inch apart. "I need a teensy-weensy favor."

Angelique sat back in her chair. "Which would be?"

"Can you stay and help us out with ideas?" So Kimberly wouldn't be alone with Ross any longer than necessary.

"I'll try to think of something while I'm in the shower, because that's all the free time I have right now. You know there's not many things I wouldn't do for you, including taking a bullet or throwing myself in front of a train, but I'm pretty bogged down at the moment." Angelique tapped a thick file that was sitting on her desk. "I have this big case coming up, and we need the money. Clients get pretty tight-fisted this time of year and don't always pay their bills until after the holidays."

So true. Angelique was the real money maker between the two of them because Kimberly handled more of the pro bono side of the firm or the clients who didn't have much income to spare, which was the nature of her chosen legal specialty. Plus, Kimberly would never want to take up Ang's time that could be spent with her young kids.

Kimberly knew all too well what it was like to be neglected by parents, especially during the holidays.

She held out her hand and waggled all five fingers. "Gimme some of it to work on tonight when I'm watching television in bed alone on a Friday night with cold cream on my face and curlers in my hair because, yes, that's how pathetic my life is."

Angelique peered over the rim of her glasses again with a deadpan stare.

"Seriously." Kimberly softened her tone. "I love you enough not to let you suffer alone. I'll work on whatever you need tonight when I'm done meeting with Ross." She shrugged. "I also have the weekend free to help out with the case, because, you know, the pathetic life and all."

Angelique thumbed through the file and withdrew a small stack of papers. She placed them in Kimberly's hands. "I need an outline for a brief. I can draft the full document myself, but it would hurry the process along and help tremendously if you can come up with bullet points for the argument I need to make to the court."

"Done. In return, stop getting it on in the shower with Dr. Tall, Dark, and Hotsome so you really can help me think up creative ideas that don't cost a lot of money." Kimberly walked away, stopping in the doorway to look over her shoulder. "Now, about that flogging. Have you seen my cat o' nine tails laying around anywhere?"

Because she was likely going to need it to remind herself to resist the allure of Ross's rugged scruff, sparkling eyes, and nicely filled-out mechanic's coveralls.

CHAPTER FOUR

Ross turned the wrench one more time, withdrew his head from under the hood of the car he was working on, and glanced at the clock hanging above a massive red tool box.

Quittin' time.

He pulled a red rag from the pocket of his coveralls and wiped the grease from his hands.

He had just enough time to get cleaned up, place an order for takeout, then join Kimberly at her office to start working on a plan, code named *How the Petite Blonde Grinch Almost Stole Christmas.*

He chuckled and tossed the rag into the laundry bin filled with more greasy rags.

Finally, he had a good excuse to spend time with her. Maybe even find out why she'd withdrawn from him several months ago, just as their relationship had felt like it was going somewhere beyond palling around.

He slammed the hood of the classic Thunderbird—shipped to him from an out-of-state client because classic cars were his specialty—and locked up the shop to head home. Dusk turned the snow-covered mountains lavender as he trod across the street to *Papa Bear's Lodge.* Every cabin on the premises twinkled with big, old fashioned Christmas lights in multi-colors, the same way his parents had decorated the lodge every year when Ross and Noelle were growing up.

Until they'd lost her, and his parents had stopped decorating at all.

Sadness crept from his chest into his stomach and formed a knot. Always did when he thought of his parents' attempt to cover their grief by erasing reminders of Noelle.

Ross usually stopped by to check in with the reception desk clerk after work. Not today. Instead, he veered right and followed the snow-packed road that twisted and turned through the rental cabins dotting the grounds. Then he headed to his own cabin—the home he and Noelle had grown up in—that sat nestled in a grove of ponderosa pines on the back of the lodge's property, where the river butted up against his back yard.

He found himself whistling. Hurrying. Anticipating.

As though tonight was a date with Kimberly.

Which it wasn't, as much as he'd wanted it to be, before she'd doused Red River's Christmas cheer with a bucket of Grinch-green water.

Maybe this was his chance to figure out why she'd pretty much ended their friendship in the first place, because he had no idea. Things had been stellar between them. They'd started as buddies, sharing the occasional beer, frequent dances, and a lot of laughs at Joe's every weekend when she drove in from Taos to spend time in Red River with her best friend. Once he and Kimberly became good friends, they'd paired up at community functions or social gatherings when everyone else had dates, spouses, or partners.

One evening at Joe's, she'd had a little too much to drink and their dancing got more intimate. Sexy as hell, even. He'd been attracted to her for some time, but had let their relationship unfold slowly. Had let their bond build gradually because he'd gotten to know her well enough to be sure she didn't let a lot of people into her inner circle.

He had no idea who'd hurt her, but he was one thousand

percent sure someone had. If he ever met the douche, Ross would love to give him some pointers on how to treat a woman. Especially a woman as special as Kimberly.

Of course, Ross had to somehow convince her to drop the Grinch act because he could never get close to someone who'd rather skip Christmas altogether.

Twenty minutes later, he'd showered, changed into fresh clothes, and was firing up his vintage Ford pickup that he'd restored himself. He worked the gear shift on the steering column, the old truck's snow tires kicking up fresh powder as he followed the path and turned left onto Main Street to pick up their dinner and a six pack of cold beer.

By the time he climbed the stairs and used a knuckle to knock on the door of *Barbetta-Holloway & Perez,* darkness had blanketed Red River, and the town's twinkling lights resembled a pouch full of diamonds that had been scattered across a sheet of snowy white velvet.

The door flew open, and Kimberly stood there in the same mismatched clothes she'd been wearing at the meeting. "Hey." Creases formed across her forehead. "Why did you knock? This is an office, not a private residence."

He gave both the warm pizza box and the cold beer a boost, one then the other, like a teeter-totter. "My hands are full. I couldn't open the door."

"Oh." She grabbed a handful of his jacket sleeve and tugged him into the foyer. "Well, then shut up and get in here before my pizza gets cold," she said in that bold, bodacious personality he adored.

It was so much like his sister's. She'd lived life without any limits once they'd gotten the news that her life wouldn't be all that long. Her bright, cheerful light had been snuffed out way too soon, and the injustice of it all was something he still couldn't understand or accept.

Kimberly kicked the door shut with one of her sequined boots and scooped the pizza box out of his hand. "I'll get plates while you undress."

He choked out a cough.

"Uh, excuse me?" he managed to ask between a strangled wheeze and a gasp for air.

She skidded to a halt. "Leave your jacket and gloves on a hook." She pointed to a coat rack next to the door. "Unless you're planning to sit through our working dinner in your winter gear? The heat's on, but I can crank it up more if you're that cold."

"No, I'll be fine. I just thought—" Another round of choked hacking had him clearing his throat behind a fisted hand.

Her big hazel eyes turned to saucers. Then pink seeped into her cheeks. "You thought I meant..." She snorted and slapped a hand against her slender thigh. "As if." Another snort.

Well, hell. He'd be offended if he didn't find her usual snorting and bluntness a turn on. It was wonderfully refreshing. Honest and down to earth. Qualities he rarely found in people, but she wore them like a badge of honor.

"I knew what you meant." He totally hadn't. "Go find plates." He waved her off. "The pizza isn't going to stay warm forever."

"Okay, okay." She sliced a hand through the air and marched out of the foyer. "Don't be a bully."

He stared at her as she disappeared down the hall, his chest tightening. She'd just said she'd never consider getting undressed with him, in not so many words. Yet his gut instincts told him that wasn't entirely true. This unique woman with all of her spunky talk and eccentric clothes—the one he'd started falling for several months ago before she doused his hopes and cut ties and run—was a puzzle. The Grinch routine, over a holiday that brought most people cheer and happiness, only deepened the mystery.

"My office is the one with the hot pink walls," she shouted from another room.

Why did that not surprise him? She was the only person he knew with the nerve to decorate a professional office in hot pink.

She yelled another command. "Make yourself useful and open us a beer."

Ross shook his head, chuckling under his breath, and went looking for her office. It was kinda hard to miss because she hadn't exaggerated when she'd mentioned the color of the walls.

They were the loudest color of pink he'd ever seen. A deep purple sofa was flanked by two chairs in the shape of giant hands. The chairs were such bright shades of blue and yellow that he'd bet they glowed in the dark. Her desk was across the room, with bookcases on each side. One wall had been converted into a giant chalkboard with childlike drawings all over it, and above the sofa hung several framed pictures of Kimberly with different groups of kids.

The bookshelves on each side of her desk were filled with community awards from where she'd lived and practiced law before relocating her practice to Red River. Most moving, though, was the multitude of plaques from various organizations that all helped children with healthcare, food, clothing, and education. Every plague was engraved with a message of gratitude for Kimberly Perez.

Wow. He'd known she was a good person, but he'd be willing to bet a real Grinch wouldn't have plaques for community service hanging on the wall.

So, what was her beef with harmless holiday decorations?

Kimberly blew into the room, putting the pizza box, plates, and napkins on the coffee table in front of the sofa. "Like my giant chalkboard?"

"I do, actually." He joined her next to the coffee table. "A long time ago, my dad and I used the same chalkboard paint to make one for my little sister on the back of her bedroom door."

"You have a sister?" Kimberly asked, obviously surprised.

Most everyone in Red River knew that Ross's parents couldn't bear to talk about Noelle, so no one mentioned her unless Ross brought her up first. Obviously, he'd never mentioned his sister in front of Kimberly.

He nodded. "The chalkboard brings back some happy memories."

"I represent a lot of children and single moms." Kimberly walked to the wall, picked up several pieces of colorful chalk from a small basket that sat on top of a plastic table for toddlers, and sketched Wheeler Peak in all of its snow-capped glory. It was nicely drawn, a talent she'd obviously kept to herself. "The board keeps the kids occupied, and they like the bright colors I used to decorate the room."

He raised both brows and nodded. "Kids feel the same way about Christmas decorations."

"Maybe so." She made her way back to the table and opened the pizza box. "But when a kid living in poverty has to choose between decorations or a toy." She held up an index finger. "Just one toy, mind you. Or if they had to choose between pretty lights or a new pair of shoes that actually fit, I'd wager they'd choose the toy or the shoes every time." She did a rolling gesture with that index finger of hers. "The beers aren't open yet?" She snapped her fingers twice. "Come on, chop chop."

He put the six pack on the coffee table and opened two of them. "Now who's the bully?"

She served up two paper plates with extra-large slices. "Sorry, but I get a little cray-cray around the scent of pepperoni and mushroom with extra cheese. How'd you know that was my favorite?"

"We've been friends long enough for me to notice a few details." He shrugged. "At least we used to be friends. I'm not sure what changed." Even before she turned into a green furry monster.

She chewed her lip for a beat and plopped onto the sofa. "Pfttt." She waved a hand in the air. "Nothing's changed." She swiped her bottle of beer off the table and chugged. Then she wiped the back of her hand across her plump lips. "Of course nothing's changed. Why would you think things have changed?"

"For starters, the rambling is a dead giveaway that you're not telling the truth and things really are different between us." Ross took a seat next to her on the sofa. "And lastly, we used to be tight but now you avoid me like I've got body odor or bad breath," he teased. Something in their relationship had definitely shifted, even before she turned into a Grinch. He stuffed his mouth with pizza before he blurted his thoughts.

"I'm an attorney. I get paid to ramble," she said. "Plus, it's been my experience that you can't rely on most people to stick around forever. That's why I don't rely on anyone but myself ... and sometimes Ang." Kimberly sliced a hand through the air. "But that's it, and I don't even rely on her very often because she actually has a life that I don't want to disrupt." Her leg bounced. "So don't take it to heart. I haven't been around because I've been busy helping people with legal problems." The bouncing got faster. "Let's find a different topic. A better topic, like how the heck are we going to decorate the whole flipping town?"

"We'll get to that in a sec." He took a pull from his longneck bottle of beer. "I was looking at all of your accolades. Pretty impressive." He pointed to the plaques and pictures. "Why didn't you ever mention the volunteer work you did before you moved your practice here? Seems like you were a big deal in that community." He bit into the extra cheesy slice, and his taste buds practically moaned with pleasure.

She shrugged, chewing on a mouthful of pizza. She washed it down with a swig of beer. "If you have to tell people you're important, then you're not."

Humility. He liked that in a person.

"Which means I don't want to talk about that either." She stared at the label of her beer bottle. "I display those because they were gifts of gratitude, not because I'm full of myself, so next question."

"What's with wanting to cancel Christmas when kids love it so much, and you obviously love kids?" It was a fair question. At least *he* thought so.

Her torso went ramrod straight.

Obviously, she disagreed.

"I've yet to meet a child of any age who doesn't love sparkling tinsel and shiny decorations," he said, trying to convince her they were on the same team.

She tried to blurt out an exasperated response around a mouthful of pizza, then slammed a hand over her mouth.

He patted her shoulder. "Calm down before you choke to death."

She chewed, glaring at him the whole time. When she was done, she said through gritted teeth, "I did not try to cancel Christmas." She pointed to the plaques. "I wanted to do more for kids than just decorate a town with flashy decorations." She pushed off the sofa. "You know what? Never mind. There's no sense trying to explain something I've already explained a bazillion times." She went and got a notepad and a pen from her desk. "We should get to work, because I'm sure we both have other places we'd rather be."

No, there really wasn't any place else he'd rather be than right there with Kimberly.

Kinda pathetic now that he thought about it.

He ran his fingers through his hair. "Okay, look. We both want good things, and arguing about who's right and who's wrong won't help either of us." She may not see the value of the wonderment a decorated town could bring to a kid, especially one whose circumstances were unfortunate, but they were getting nowhere fast. Ross needed to change strategies. "Truce?" He held out a hand. "If we're going to work together on this, then we at least need to get along."

She stared at his hand for several beats. Then she slowly reached out and gave it a quick decisive shake. When she tried to withdraw her hand, his fingers closed around her soft creamy skin.

No idea why he did that, but he couldn't make his fingers let go.

An electric current skated up his arm.

Her big eyes snapped to his, and for a moment, he got lost in them.

"Can we be friends again, like we used to be?" His voice went gravely. Even though they were on opposite sides of an issue that he couldn't ... he wouldn't allow himself to budge on, he did care enough about Kimberly to want her as a friend.

Her eyes widened and clouded over, her look not at all matching her words of disinterest or her attitude of avoiding him lately. She swayed toward him just a fraction, but it was enough for hope to spring to life again. For the briefest of moments, he thought she'd lean in and kiss him because her lips parted, and the tip of her tongue slipped through to trace the seam of her mouth.

He didn't move.

Her gaze skimmed over his face. Dropped to his mouth. Lingered there for a long time.

"Kimberly," he finally whispered.

A dull throb beat against his chest when she straightened and leaned away from him.

He released her hand.

"Um, sure," she said. "Friends. Like we've always been." She picked up her pad and clicked the pen open and closed several times. "We've got work to do, so let's get to it."

Two hours, three beers each, and a full pizza later, they had the framework to accomplish their task. Wasn't going to be easy, but they could do it because he had the brawn and she had the brains.

She walked him to the door, and he pulled on his jacket.

"I'll pick you up in the morning." The zipper of his down jacket whizzed as he pulled it up to his neck. "Dress warm and wear snow boots." He let one side of his mouth lift into a lopsided grin and pointed to her sequined boots. "Not those. They're not made for breaking a trail through fresh snow."

"Why would we be breaking a trail? I thought we were going to get a pine for the Wishing Tree?" Her mouth gaped.

"We are, but the best place to get a tree is pretty remote." He pulled on his gloves.

"There are tons of trees for sale in front of the hardware store," she insisted. "No trail breaking necessary."

He pulled his knit winter cap on. "They're not big enough for the park, and even if they were, they'd be too expensive. I know where we can get a big one free of charge." He opened the door.

"But it's just you and me. How will we get it back to town?" She followed him onto the landing.

He started down the stairs without looking back. "Let me worry about that. I'll pick you up in the morning at eight AM sharp."

She blew out a heavy breath. "I'll be here at the office, waiting out front."

He waved an *okay* over one shoulder. The tree was going to be a snap. Tamping down both his attraction to Kimberly, not to mention his frustration with her, weren't going to be so easy.

CHAPTER FIVE

The next morning, Kimberly waited on the icy sidewalk outside her office for Ross to pick her up so they could find a Wishing Tree for the park. She pressed a ball point pen to the clipboard in her hand and checked off step one of their to-do list with sparkly purple ink.

The sooner they got to the end of the list the better. Once the last step was complete, they could both get back to their real responsibilities, which were a lot more important than silly decorations.

How she'd had the energy to pull herself out of a warm bed and get ready on time was beyond her. She'd sat up most of the night to work on Angelique's brief and send out emails to charitable organizations that might help create a list of kids who could put their wishes on the tree.

Never mind that once Kimberly finally went to bed, she'd stared at the ceiling the rest of the night thinking of how Ross had accused her, *again,* of trying to rob Red River of a real Christmas. Of how he'd asked why their friendship had changed. Of how heat had pounded through her veins when she'd put her hand in his to shake on a truce, but then he'd held on longer than a platonic friendship called for.

Firm, but gentle. Professional, but sensual.

A shiver raced over her.

It was the cold winter temperatures.

It certainly was not the thought of him stroking the pad of his thumb over the back of her hand.

Nopity, nope, nope.

That had no effect on her whatsoever.

She stuffed the clipboard under an arm and blew into her gloved hands. Frosty mist swirled into the air.

Where *was* that hunk of a man, anyway? She was freezing her ta-tas off. That was saying something because she'd been blessed with a sizable rack, if she did say so herself.

At that early hour on a Saturday morning, the streets of Red River were pretty empty. Besides a snow plow working its way in her direction, Main Street was quiet. Not even the ski lifts had opened yet, and the empty chairs swayed gently in the breeze. Rays of early morning sunshine peaked over the jagged mountain tops, making the fresh powder that had fallen overnight glisten like precious jewels.

If it weren't for her teeth chattering and her limbs going numb, she might actually enjoy the peacefulness before the shops started to open and the town came to life.

Just about every shop on Main Street had decorated for Christmas on their own. Every window had a Christmas scene painted onto it, lights, and holiday trim in the windows. What difference would a few more decorations hanging on the street lamps, around the gazebo, and in the park make? Kimberly still didn't see the reasoning behind it, or why Red River couldn't go without Ms. Francine's industrial sized balls.

Kimberly snorted, sending a cloud of frosty mist rushing into the air.

The snow plow drew closer, but the sound of a diesel engine coming from the other end of Main Street pierced through the plow's *swish, swish, swishing,* and she stood on tippey-toes to see who it was. What looked like Ross's heavy-duty work truck, that he used to tow some of the automobiles he worked on, puttered along, pulling a flatbed trailer in its wake.

Thank God he was finally on his way, but dang. If they were going to get a tree big enough to need a trailer and a winch, then they were likely going to need more muscle than just the two of them.

As he got closer, she could make out his squared jaw and aviator sunglasses through the front windshield.

She straightened her knit cap, smoothed a palm over her jacket. Then looked down her length at her color coordinated outfit and went stock-still.

Even her teeth stopped chattering.

Ross had told her to dress in snow gear. Her matching black winter pants, black faux fur-lined snow boots, black jacket with purple piping along the edges, black hat and gloves, black *everything* must've been a subconscious effort to win over the local business owners she planned to visit after they were done finding a tree. Half the town was angry at her, so she had to make a good impression when she walked into the shops along Main Street and asked them to support the Wishing Tree by taking a child's wish for a gift and making it come true.

Her conservative wardrobe choice, which actually matched for a change, certainly wasn't to dazzle Ross Armstrong.

Just as he pulled up next to the curb across the street and rolled down his window, the snow plow passed between them.

Icy slush sprayed all over her.

The shock of it caused her to haul in a breath and hold it. Eyes closed, mouth hanging open, arms out.

The sound of the plow started to fade before she finally opened her eyes and looked down at the mess on her clothes.

"Are you okay?" He propped an elbow on the doorframe, the top half of his body leaning out of the open window.

She wiped a chunk of slush from under one eye and shook it off her fingers. "I'm perfect. A splash of icy snow is exactly how I prefer to start my day."

One side of his mouth cocked up into a lazy smile. Even though he wore shades, she knew the humor that sparkled in his green eyes when he joked with her was there. "You didn't hear the snow plow coming?"

Yes, she damn sure had heard it. In the background of her thoughts, that had been focused more on Ross and her absurdly coordinated clothing than on an approaching snow plow.

She brushed off the front of her jacket, the whiteish gray snow a stark contrast to her black gear. "I was deep in thought about our to-do list." She dusted off her pants.

"Hop in and get out of the cold." He watched her. "Normally, when I pick up a lady, I wouldn't ask her to cross the street." He hooked a thumb toward the trailer. "But I can't be as chivalrous pulling this thing."

"Then it's a good thing I'm not one of your ladies, so you don't have to worry about chivalry."

His smile faded.

She jogged across the street and slid into the passenger seat. "I'm one of the guys. No chivalry needed."

He rolled up his window, shifted gears, and pulled away from the curb. "Call me old-fashioned, but I'm a gentleman to women, whether I'm dating them or not." He grabbed one of the two insulated tumblers from the console cupholders. "Sorry, I'm a few minutes late. I made fresh coffee for both of us."

She took it and let the warm liquid slide down her throat. She made a refreshed sound, as though she was starring in a soda commercial. "Now, that's the kind of chivalry I like. Thank you." She went to take another drink.

In a flash, a big furry head popped over her shoulder from the back seat and licked a big, sloppy tongue up her cheek.

She screamed, plastering herself against the door. Coffee sloshed all over her clothes.

Oh, for God's sake.

"*Comet*," Ross scolded. He hooked a finger under the giant beast's collar and pulled it away from her. "Sit."

It whined and disappeared from between the front seats.

"Holy cow," Kimberly breathed out, her head falling back against the seat. "I thought Cujo had me." Her heart pounded against her ribcage.

"He's a Golden Retriever mix I just rescued. He's harmless." Ross fumbled around in the console, then handed her a rag. "Sorry about the mess."

She dabbed at the beads of coffee dotting her jacket, then wiped her cheek and peeked around the seat at the panting dog. "He's wearing Christmas antlers." Just like Max, the Grinch's dog.

Ross lifted a shoulder. "I couldn't resist."

"Please tell me he already had that name when you rescued him." Cleaned off, she took another drink of what was left of her coffee.

"He didn't have a name." Ross hesitated. "Comet seemed to fit since I got him so close to Christmas." A muscle in his strong jaw twitched.

"Oh, my *gawd*." She gasped, placing a hand over her mouth. "You're one of those holiday freaks who lives for Christmas all year long, aren't you?" She didn't wait for an answer because he deserved to get as well as he gave for the Grinch antlers. "Do you play Christmas music in July?" When he didn't respond, she fake-slugged him on the arm. "You do!"

"You're gonna make me crash." He pretended to swerve off the road because of the tap she delivered to his arm. "And I do not listen to Christmas carols in July. I wait until September at least."

She snorted with satisfaction.

A silky, golden brow arched above the rim of his shades. "At least I'm not one of those freaks who wants nothing to do with the holiday season at all." He reached for the stereo system on the dash, and a Christmas jingle filled the cab.

"*Awww,* you're a Christmas sap," she teased in a voice she usually reserved for Angelique's darling little children. "That's so cute."

Because it *was* pretty adorable. And sweet. And sexy as hell.

He turned the music louder and started humming the tune.

"That was a compliment," she yelled over the stereo.

"Right," he said without lowering the volume. "Every man wants to be called cute." He let out a sharp whistle and the dog's head appeared between the seats. "Comet, give her a kiss." He patted Kimberly's shoulder.

"No—" A gigantic tongue left a trail of wetness across her cheek, and she pressed her back against the door, holding up the tumbler as a barrier to fend off the furry thing. "Okay, okay. I take it back. You're not cute."

"Down, Comet." At Ross's command, the dog stopped licking her but kept his big head between the front seats, with his tongue lolling out one side of his mouth.

"Eww." She picked up the rag, wiped her face, then wadded it into a ball and tossed it at Ross's head.

"What?" He tried to sound innocent, but the corner of his mouth curved.

She shook her head. "I'm not used to dogs. Especially dogs with big slobbery tongues."

"Cats?" he asked, yielding as the road leading out of Red River merged onto the highway.

"Nope." She patted Comet's head, then shooed him to the back seat before the big lug ended up in her lap.

"What kind of person doesn't like pets *or* Christmas?" He used a playful tone, but his words still pricked at a hole in her heart that had never been filled. Likely, it never would be.

"The kind who grew up in foster homes and knows better than to get attached to things."

His subtle, smart-assy smile slid away. "Oh." He turned the music down. "I never knew that, Kimberly. How come you never told me?"

Why would she do that? "Because I don't need your pity, so stop it. Your voice is dripping with it."

"It's called compassion, not pity." Ross draped a hand over the steering wheel. "Of all the people I know, you're the last one I'd pity."

Well, hells bells. "Now I'm offended."

"You shouldn't be." He shook his head. "*That* was a compliment. You don't need pity. You're so ... competent and comfortable in your own skin."

Her head snapped around to study him. For someone who rarely found herself at a loss for words or a witty comeback, she had nothin'. The awkward silence filling the cab was as thick as fresh hip-deep snow.

So she decided to lighten the mood. "Tell me what kind of guy goes ga-ga over Christmas?" She laugh-snorted. "I mean, you even named your dog after a selfish reindeer who likely bullied a less popular reindeer because of a shiny nose."

Even with shades on, she could tell the look he shot her was wry.

Aaaaand the friendly banter was back.

"Fine," she said. "Maybe Comet wasn't a bully. Maybe Comet was one of the nice reindeer who wanted to let Rudolph join in the games." Come to think of it, she was a lot like Rudolph. A misfit who tried to use her painful past as a motivator instead of an excuse.

When Ross didn't respond, she said, "Okay, I'll stop cracking jokes and be serious. I really want to know why you're so crazy about Christmas."

He shook his head. "No, you don't."

"Sure, I do." She leaned against the door and studied him. "I don't meet a lot of guys who go all out for Christmas, so I'm curious."

The muscle in his jaw tensed and didn't release. Finally, he drew in a deep breath. "It's a family tradition that my sister started a long time ago. Now I carry it on for her."

Oh.

A family tradition.

Kimberly could picture it as clearly as she could see the snowy winter landscape through her window. Ross as a young boy with his family. Presents under a twinkling tree they were dying to unwrap. The aroma of a special meal wafting from the kitchen.

Kimberly had experienced exactly zero of that growing up, until she finally was taken under the wing of Angelique's big Italian family when they'd met in law school. The loud Barbetta clan treated her like one of their own, but still, she'd never gotten over feeling like an outsider. An interloper.

Tears pricked the back of her eyes, and she forced herself to swallow back the gravel in her mouth.

"That..." Her voice went croaky, and she cleared her throat. "That's a good reason." Any hint of the snark she and Ross usually volleyed back and forth was gone. Instead, her voice was almost a whisper. "Really, I'm sure your memories of the holidays with your family are lovely."

Ross glanced at her and sighed. "Told you that you wouldn't want to know. I figured it would make you sad ... if you grew up in..."

He obviously didn't know how to finish without making her feel worse.

She waved him off. Shook her head but couldn't speak. She kept her mouth clamped shut for the rest of the drive and stared straight ahead. She could not let herself cry over not having family traditions. Not having *holiday* family traditions.

If that dam ever broke, she wasn't sure she'd be able to stop the flood of emotions that would likely flow like a raging river. Those emotions ran so deep that they would surely pull her under and never let her surface for air.

Keeping them bottled up had been her coping mechanism while growing up. She'd just have to stuff a gigantic cork in the bottle, too, because she wasn't going to let silly emotions from the past break her.

Ever.

CHAPTER SIX

"No. Freaking. Way." Kimberly clutched the *oh shit* bar over the passenger window of Ross's truck as he pulled to a stop deep in the woods because the road—if one could really call it that—had ended. "When you pulled off the highway, I thought we were going to a tree farm to find a Wishing Tree." Not to the flipping wilderness. "Where *are* we?"

Ross killed the engine. "It's a tree farm of sorts. It's my land, and I got up before day break to plow the road so we could get this far. We'll have to walk the rest of the way."

He got out and shut the door before she could protest, so she did the same.

"Did you bring bread crumbs?" She pointed at the dense forest. "If we get lost in there, they won't find our lifeless bodies until the spring thaw." No wonder he'd told her to dress warm and wear real winter boots instead of her sequined Uggs.

Which reminded her...

"You seriously expect us to break a trail through that?" She pointed to a clearing off to the left that glistened with untouched snow. Considering the amount of snow that had already fallen that season, knee-deep was probably a conservative estimate. "My lungs hurt already."

He reached over the side of his truck and retrieved two pairs of snowshoes. "That's why I brought these." He came around to her side of the truck and opened the passenger door. "Hop in. I'll help you put them on." He slid his aviators to rest on top of his head.

She climbed back into the passenger seat, letting her legs dangle out of the open door.

Ross went down on a knee.

For a moment, Kimberly's heart fluttered. Her tummy flip-flopped.

Her uterus—the little hussy—quivered.

If she and Ross were in love, she'd swear he was about to propose, and the thought made her brain go fuzzy and her insides fill with emotions she didn't understand. Had never wanted to understand, because that meant having to count on someone other than herself.

They absolutely were not in love, though. Nor would they ever be. So, Ladyland—the traitorous witch she obviously was—could go back into hibernation and stop putting ridiculous thoughts into Kimberly's head.

Ross took her foot and studied it, his gentleness a tell-tell sign of the kind of guy he was. Burly and brawny, but gentle and considerate.

"You have big feet for such a little person." He slid the snowshoe onto her boot, tightening the straps.

Um. Okay.

She bit down on her tongue to force herself back to reality.

"Thanks for pointing that out. It's every gal's dream to be told they have big feet. Kind of like calling a guy cute."

"Sorry." He reached for her other foot. "I just meant that my sister's snowshoes will fit you better than I thought because she had big feet, too, like me."

Kimberly went quiet. His sister *had* big feet, as in past tense?

Seemed like Kimberly wasn't the only one holding back painful experiences from the past.

Ross finished securing the straps, but instead of getting up, he held onto her ankle. His touch was tender. Through a pair of thermals, snow pants, and boots!

Kimberly's heart thrummed.

His gaze traveled up her length all the way to her knit cap. "You look nice, by the way."

Involuntarily, she ran a hand over her winter cap. "You noticed. Most guys don't."

"I'm not most guys," he said.

Didn't she know it.

He stood, bracing a hand against the top of the doorframe, and leaned closer. "I gotta say, Kimberly, you don't usually dress like this, so is the new look for me?"

She scoffed. "*No.*"

His expression went stony.

"I've got to brave the fiery darts of hell that are likely going to be thrown at me when I personally visit every business in town as soon as we're done here. I wanted to make a good impression."

He gave her a skeptical look.

Or maybe it was disappointment.

"I do the same to impress a judge. Do you think I show up in court wearing sequined boots?" She shook her head. "I wear conservative power suits." She pursed her lips to keep from mentioning that she always put on bright unconventional lingerie under those suits, because *hello,* she had to stay true to herself somehow. "I have a total of *two* suits; one black and one navy."

Creases formed above his brows. "I guess I never considered how you dress for court." Then he smiled. "I'd really love to see you trying to look conservative in one of those suits with that hair."

She let her eyes bug out at the pseudo insult. "I'll have you know that most people love my hair." Not really, but whatever. She ran a hand over her cap again, even though her hair was completely covered except for the tips. "But I do comb it flat instead of wearing it wild when I go to court. It's in my clients' best interest to assimilate."

"And I'll have *you* know that I'm one of the people who love your hair. It suits your personality," he said. "I'm also impressed that making the Wishing Tree a success for the kids means so much to you that you'd dress out of character for it."

Oh. Well, okay.

"I'll have a long list of wishes for the tree within a few days. So I need every business and resident in Red River to take one of those wishes and make it come true. Otherwise, it'll be just another disappointment for children who have likely already suffered way too many disappointments in their young lives."

Silence filled the air as he studied her, as though he was seeing her for the first time.

Red flag. Had she said too much? Just enough for him to get a glimpse of how damaged she was from her pathetic upbringing?

She scrunched her nose. "Why on earth did you buy land way out here, when you have a perfectly nice cabin at the lodge?"

He pulled in a breath and looked around, taking in his property. "I figured I'd want to start a family some day, and this would be a really nice place to build a house and raise kids."

Her breath caught in her chest.

Kids. Family. A home, instead of just a house.

She couldn't take much more. Ross was great husband material for someone who actually wanted a husband. He'd make an even better father, she'd bet. The thought of him swinging little kids, who looked just like him, on a swing set, then climbing into bed with his wife at the end of the day ... a wife who definitely would not have the name Kimberly Perez...

Well, it made her feel even more empty.

"Well, good for you. I'll come to the wedding when you meet Mrs. Right." She pushed on his shoulders. "Come on, big guy. Do your lumberjack routine and go kill an innocent tree just to save Christmas for Red River."

He knelt and went to work on his own shoes. "I plant five saplings for every tree I cut down."

Of course he did. It was impossible to find even the smallest thing to dislike about Ross. Which was why she'd played the disappearing game several months ago, and made herself scarce when he was around town.

When he was done with his shoes, he let out a sharp whistle that pierced through the cold air.

Comet bounded over the console into the front seat and placed a paw on each of Kimberly's shoulders. His big chops rested on top of her head.

Ross belly laughed. "Perfect." He reached inside his pocket and retrieved a phone. "I have to have a picture of this. It's going on my desk as one of my favorite Christmas memories, right next to the last Christmas I was able to spend with my sister, Noelle."

For a moment, all the joy melted from his eyes, his mouth, his very countenance.

Her name was *Noelle?* There had to be a sad story there, and it must've been the reason he went crazy over Christmas. And Kimberly had teased him for it. "I'm so sorry for your loss."

And just like that, he was back to the old Ross, snapping off pictures with a smile. "It's fine. *This* makes it okay, because it's exactly the kind of thing that would've made her happy. Come on, Grinch, smile for the camera."

Kimberly rolled her eyes, then struck a pose. Then she circled her arms behind her head and around Comet's neck. The dog whimpered, and when she looked up at him, the damned thing licked her right on the mouth.

Kimberly crinkled up her entire face, but she couldn't bring herself to pull away, because this was obviously Ross's way of paying tribute to the sister he'd lost. "Eww!" Kimberly clamped her eyes shut and let Comet cover her face with sloppy kisses. She gave Ross an *I give up* look while the dog had his way with her ear.

Ross clicked off more pictures, then stared at his phone with a frown. "I guess the cold got to it because it just shut down." He put the phone away and started toward Kimberly.

"Then can you get your dog off me?" Kimberly patted Comet on the head. "Between the French kiss and the wet willy he gave me, he's already gotten to second base. That's further than I've let any guy go since..." Her voice trailed off at the look in Ross's eyes as he advanced on her.

He stopped in front of her, lips parted, eyes smoky. "Since when, Kimberly?" If she'd thought the deep tenor of his voice was sexy before, the huskiness that vibrated through it now was panty-melting hot.

"Um." The tip of her tongue slipped through her parted lips to trace the seam. "What?"

"How long has it been?" Ross placed a gloved hand on each of her thighs and smoothed them up to her hips.

"Wh...why?" She tried to shimmy backward, but Comet was in the way. "I mean, it's not like it's any of your business." She gave him a friendly slug to the arm. "Right, big guy?" Then she snorted out a fake laugh.

His eyes wandered over her face and anchored to her mouth. Frosty breaths filled the small space between them, their noses almost touching. "I suppose it's not, but I wouldn't mind making it my business. So, how long?"

She nibbled on her bottom lip. "Um, well," she whispered. "I'm having something of a dry spell."

Who was she kidding? Her sex life was like the Mojave.

At the moment, Ross Armstrong strongly resembled an oasis that was calling to her for a long, refreshing drink.

"I could help you out with that," he murmured. "If you wanted me to."

Heat zinged through her veins.

He placed a finger under her chin and lifted her gaze to his, their eyes locking.

It was the simplest, yet the most intimate of gestures. His touch and his eyes both communicated a softness that Kimberly had never known. Never *let* herself experience because it couldn't last. If a man could actually get past the crazy clothes, wild hair, and flamboyant personality—which were there to keep men out to begin with—they wouldn't want her once they saw underneath the façade.

Kimberly didn't do rejection. She'd had enough of that to last two lifetimes, and she'd never give anyone that kind of power over her emotions again.

Yet in that moment, maybe one kiss wouldn't hurt. Maybe a kiss from a man who looked at her as though he wanted to give her much more.

Before she knew what she was doing, she gave her head a tiny nod.

Ross let out a low throaty growl, then he took her mouth with his.

Red hot fire arrowed straight to her core, and she moaned. *Moaned!*

Which made him growl again and crush his lips harder to hers, wrapping her in his arms. Her lips parted, and she snaked her arms around his neck.

His tongue—his wonderful, glorious tongue—swooped in and took charge. Not gentle this time, but demanding and driven with need.

She sighed into his mouth and melted into him.

He framed her face with both hands and angled her head, then deepened the kiss, bringing it to surface-of-the-sun hot.

Her desire spiked, crashing through her to drown out the voice in the back of her mind that told her this wasn't a good idea.

When she slid both hands under his jacket to warm them against his flannel shirt, he groaned.

Comet barked.

They pulled apart, and Kimberly touched her swollen lips with her fingertips.

Ross closed his eyes and leaned his forehead against hers. "Can we pick this up later tonight?" He chuckled. "Preferably indoors, where it's warm?" He glanced around her. "And where I can give Comet a bone and shut him in the pantry for a while."

"Look, Ross—"

"Tonight." He stepped away and withdrew a chainsaw out of

the back of his truck. "We either continue this or you tell me why we can't, because we both obviously want it to happen. Either way, it's your choice." He stepped over a bank of untouched snow and started breaking a trail. "The tree I've got in mind isn't that far, so follow me."

Comet whined at her back, so she slid out of the truck and took a few steps to get used to the snowshoes.

The dog bounded out of the truck, with his antlers bouncing around, and followed Ross.

Ross was someone she wished she could follow, too, and not just through the snow but through life. She'd given up on that dream a long time ago, though. Resolved in her heart that it was better to be alone than to be let down, or worse, end up disappointing someone like him.

He'd labeled her a Grinch. Maybe that's exactly what she'd be if it meant saving him from herself.

CHAPTER SEVEN

Chopping down and transporting a huge tree all by their lone-somes hadn't been as difficult as Kimberly thought it would be. Ross had tied down the branches so they wouldn't break, used the winch attached to the front of his truck to drag it to the road where they'd been parked, then hoisted it onto the flatbed trailer with a mini-crane, which was built into the bed of his truck.

And *voila*. Pretty impressive.

Not nearly as impressive as the kiss he'd laid on her, though.

As they drove back to town, she kept quiet, giving one-word answers or nods to his questions and comments. Finally, she reached over and turned up the radio, found a hard rock station, and played the headbanger music so loud there was no way they could have carried on a conversation.

Without a word, Ross switched it to a softer station.

She switched it back to rock and roll.

He let out an exasperated sigh, and his lips pinched. He turned off the radio altogether and guarded the on-off switch with one hand.

To say the silence inside the truck had been awkward was an understatement.

Mission more than accomplished. She'd wanted to act the Grinch to push him away so he wouldn't have false hope, and she'd achieved that in spades.

Which made her feel like the brown pile Comet had left steaming out in the snow-white wilderness.

She got out her clipboard, flipped to a blank page and started to doodle. Before she knew it, she'd sketched a picture of Comet wearing his annoying antlers.

Ross took his eyes off the road just long enough to see her drawing. "Nice. Where did you learn to draw like that?"

She flipped the other pages back over the top of the clipboard to cover her sketch. "Nowhere. It was just something I started doing when I was a kid to stay busy when there were no toys or video games available." Hell, many of her foster homes hadn't had sufficient heating in the winter, cooling in the summer, or even food on a daily basis. When she could find a piece of paper and a pen or pencil, it had been like striking gold.

"You must've been born with natural talent, because you're good at it." Ross coasted to a stop in front of the park.

"It's just chicken scratch." She waved him off dismissively.

He pinched the bridge of his nose, as if to say he was at the end of his rope with her.

A group of brawny men stood in a circle chatting it up next to the gazebo.

"I texted them before we started back to town." Ross put the truck into park and killed the engine. "They're here to help set up the tree."

"Wow, Ross. You've got superpowers with that contacts list of yours." She let out a friendly chuckle. Not her usual full-on snort, but enough of a laugh to try and lighten the mood. "They're like our own personal elves."

Apparently, he didn't appreciate her smartassery. Without responding, he got out of the truck, called Comet to follow, and slammed the door a little harder than she'd expected.

She put a palm against her forehead. Pushing him away was one thing. Pissing him off so royally was quite another. A nice guy like Ross didn't deserve that kind of treatment.

She grabbed her clipboard and opened her door. She stopped. Tapped her pen against the paper on top. What could it hurt to leave him a memento of their Christmas decorating expedition? Because when it was over, she didn't plan on spending time with him anymore. Didn't plan on giving him false hope. She flipped to Comet's portrait, tore it out and left it on the dash. Then she went around to the rear of the trailer, where Ross was loosening the straps over the tree.

The group of helpers were strolling toward the curb.

"Listen, big guy," she said, unable to stop fidgeting.

Without looking up or even acknowledging her presence, Ross kept loosening the straps that held the tree in place.

His team of helpers got closer, and she knew there wasn't enough time to smooth things over, so she had to talk fast. "You seem to have this part handled, so I'm going to start working on the rest of our list." She tapped the clipboard.

Still no answer.

She heaved out a breath. "I'll..." The group of men was almost to the edge of the park. "I'll check in with you later so we can give Ms. Clydelle an update on our progress."

When he gave her a nod that was barely noticeable, she turned and walked toward the nearest strip of offices so she could start gathering supporters for the Wishing Tree. By the time she was done, she had a long list of local businesses who were willing to make a child's Christmas wish come true.

She also had a mob of business owners who had all but threatened—with a friendly smile on their faces—to chase her out of town with pitchforks if she didn't see to it that Red River's tradition was continued by cheerfully decorating it for the holidays.

The bell over the door jingled as she left the last of the shops along Main Street and stepped onto the sidewalk. She came to an abrupt halt so as not to plow into Ms. Clydelle and Ms. Francine.

Geez, did they have a satellite radar locked onto her location?

Or maybe they'd implanted a GPS locator when she was asleep. "Um, morning, ladies." Kimberly clutched her clipboard to her chest.

"Good morning, dear." Ms. Francine's purse dangled from her arm.

"I haven't heard from you, and the town council is getting antsy." Chairperson Clydelle said it as though it was an accusation.

"I was given this assignment yesterday," Kimberly deadpanned.

"Time's a wasting." Chairperson Clydelle leaned on her cane. "It's my responsibility, as the council chair, to see to it that you follow through."

The unspoken *or else* at the end of Ms. Clydelle's sentence wasn't lost on Kimberly.

Fine. If these women wanted to play tough, they'd met their match. There was no one tougher than a kid who'd grown up bouncing around so many foster homes that she'd lost count by the time she was twelve.

"The Wishing Tree is going up in the park as we speak. I've got charitable organizations compiling a list of kids and their wishes." She boosted her clipboard. "I've just gotten commitments from more than enough volunteers to fulfill those wishes, and I'm about to slay several more items on my action plan instead of working on my outstanding legal cases." Kimberly met Ms. Clydelle's determined stare and refused to look away.

A clock must've been nearby because Kimberly swore she heard it ticking as the staring contest continued. And continued.

And continued!

A bead of perspiration trickled down her spine.

Still, Chairperson Clydelle didn't look away. Didn't offer a word of praise for what Kimberly and Ross had accomplished. Didn't offer any encouragement for how much work was still to be done in such a short amount of time.

"You look nice today, dear," Ms. Francine cooed. "Who's the lucky man?"

Unable to stop herself, Kimberly looked away from Ms.

Clydelle, glanced down at her clothes, then her gaze snapped to Ms. Francine, whose wrinkled lips had curved into a sly smile. The old woman blinked innocently behind her soda bottle lenses.

Oh, these two old hens were good.

"You don't think a gal can dress up for herself?" Kimberly kicked into cross examination mode.

Besides, anyone she thought enough of to dress up for wouldn't be considered lucky in Kimberly's opinion. She wasn't exactly a prize. If the poor schmuck didn't realize that going in, he'd figure it out soon enough. And if he didn't, then *he* was likely even less of a prize than her.

Every foster parent who had actually liked Kimberly ended up being unreliable at best.

"Oh, when we see a change in a woman..." Ms. Francine tapped a boney finger against her chin, as though she were thinking, "... like a different wardrobe for instance, it's always because they're trying to catch the attention of a man."

Kimberly's jaw hung open. "That's an outdated mindset, don't you think?"

Chairperson Clydelle waved a hand in the air. "Contrary to popular belief, human nature doesn't change. Whoever he is, don't let him distract you from your goal. Red River is counting on you." She shook her cane in Kimberly's direction. "I'll be expecting another update bright and early tomorrow morning." Her cane thumped rhythmically as the two sisters strolled away.

When Kimberly got to her office, Angelique was there.

"Hey," Kimberly said, sticking her head into Ang's office.

Angelique looked up and froze for a second. "Your clothes are different. Why?"

Kimberly threw her hands in the air, gave an exaggerated eye roll, and flung herself onto the sofa. "*Why* does *everyone* keep *saying* that?"

Angelique lifted a shoulder. "Because it's true?" She swiveled back to her keyboard. "I was about to say your mood was different today, too, but apparently it's not."

"Different how?" Kimberly rested her head against the rich leather sofa.

"Less dramatic. Less scary." Angelique went back to typing. "I was wrong."

Kimberly ignored her. "What are you doing here on the weekend?"

Angelique didn't look up from her work. "Kids caught the stomach flu. No way could I concentrate on writing this brief at home, so I came here. If I'd stayed home to work on it, I would've likely ended up subconsciously referencing projectile vomit somehow in the text. It pays to have a doctor for a husband." She used a fingertip to push her reading glasses up the bridge of her nose, then went back to typing like the wind. "Thanks for the outline, by the way. It saved my ass."

"Saved *our* asses. You're the one pulling in most of the money." Kimberly slouched down on the sofa.

Angelique stopped typing and pulled off her glasses to stare at Kimberly. "Your pro bono work is just as important as the paying clients. Those charitable cases are the reason our phone is ringing off the hook from new clients all over the state who *can* pay our fees, so stop acting like you don't contribute."

"Pffttt," Kimberly scoffed. "Meanwhile, I'm up to my boobs in figuring out how to decorate a town with little to no money to work with. Like that's really going to help fill our bank account with income." She rolled her eyes.

Angelique angled her head. "It might. Have you thought about contacting a few media channels in bigger cities? Tell them what you're doing with the Wishing Tree and see if they bite. You never know. There might be some big companies out there who want to get involved, and you'd be right in their sights. Sounds like good, free advertising to me. For both the decorations you need and our firm."

Kimberly pinched the corners of her eyes with a forefinger and thumb. "I didn't start any of this for free advertising, or for us to get more business out of it. I did it to help kids who grew up like

me. Somehow, it's turned into a whole lot more than that."
Besides, even if big companies were willing to buy decorations and
donate them to the cause, the decorations would still cost money
that could and should be used to help more kids. So that idea still
undermined her original intent.

Unless...

She shot off the sofa. "Thanks, Ang. I knew I could count on
you to help me with ideas."

Angelique frowned. "Um, sure?" Her expression said she had
no idea what she'd done to help.

"I might be gone for a few days. Call me if you need more
help." Kimberly went to her office and stuffed some papers and her
laptop into a briefcase so she could still get legal work done while
she was out of the office. Then she grabbed some craft supplies
that she kept around for when her clients came in with their
children.

Before she left, she sent a text to Ross.

Have business out of town. Might be gone a few days.

Before she got to the door, her phone dinged. She put down
her armful of stuff and read Ross's response.

We've got a town to decorate!!! You can't leave NOW.

She fired off another message.

*The trip is for the decorations. While I'm gone, ask around town and
collect all the used Christmas lights that people can do without. We'll recycle
those to light up the tree.*

The dots jumped, and she waited for him to respond.

Oh. OK.

She smiled and typed.

*While I'm gone, I'll be working on glittery snowflakes to hang on the
tree. The wishes will be on each one. And FOR GOD'S SAKE, check in
with Ms. Clydelle every morning while I'm gone!*

Ross's response popped onto her screen within seconds.

You're pretty smart for a Grinch.

Kimberly should be offended. She wasn't, though. If Ross was teasing her, then he couldn't be quite as pissed as he'd been during the ride back to Red River.

She scooped up her things and headed out of the office, smiling so broad and so deep that she could feel it in her soul.

Come to think of it, maybe what she felt inside was her heart growing a few sizes.

———

Ross had no idea what Kimberly was up to leaving town when they had so much more to accomplish.

He drew cold winter air into his lungs and hammered another cable into the frozen ground as several of his friends helped him erect the tree in the park.

Was she really going on a road trip to help accomplish their mission? Or was she running from him again after the hot-as-hell kiss they'd shared? Or maybe she was running away because she'd finally opened up enough for him to get a small glimpse under the flamboyant armor she wore.

He hadn't known many people who'd grown up in foster care, but he assumed most had trust issues. How could they not?

He finished securing the last of three cables to the ground where they'd cleared away the snow. The thick wires attached to the top of the tree helped keep it upright with tension. He stepped back and let the other guys take over, who were helping drive stakes through the base of the tree into the ground for extra support.

No wonder Kimberly didn't care much for the holidays. He doubted they'd been happy occasions for her.

The question was, did he really want to know what she'd been through growing up, especially if she was going to keep shutting him out over and over again? After the way she'd shunned him during the ride back to town, he should forget about it.

He pulled off his thick work gloves and stuffed them into his jacket pocket.

Truth was, he did want to know what life had been like for her when she was a kid. Maybe it would help him figure her out. Maybe she wouldn't be such a Grinch if she made new Christmas memories.

Happier Christmas memories.

One of his buddies, who was working on driving the stakes through the base of the tree, looked up, then glanced at Ross. "You've got company." He notched up his chin toward the street.

Ross looked over his shoulder, and his chest tightened.

Damn.

He hoped like hell that whatever Kimberly was off doing was worth it, because Red River's more religious residents were gathering on the far side of the park with scowls on their faces. He hadn't exactly won them to his side at the town council meeting, so dealing with them alone might not be the best strategy.

One of them waved him over.

Hell.

He had no choice but to go it alone.

"Thanks, guys," he said to the crew of men who'd answered his call for help with the tree. "I'll let you know if I need anything else."

He turned to walk across the park, Comet trailing in his wake.

No time like the present. He trudged over the snow-covered lawn in the direction of the church folks.

Truth was, it really wouldn't feel like Christmas without a Nativity scene. He just didn't know where he was going to get the money for one big enough to be noticeable.

"Morning, folks." He strolled up to the half-dozen or so crowd. "How are you this fine Saturday morning?"

To their credit, they all responded with a kind greeting, even if their expressions ranged from wary to perturbed.

"I'm Deacon West from the church over on Copper Trail. Since Jesus is the *real* reason for the season, we'd like to know if He's going to be represented in the new decorations?"

"Funny, you should ask." Ross scratched the scruff on his jaw.

"I've been trying to figure out how to make that happen on the budget we've got. I'm assuming a big one made out of material that'll last outdoors will be pretty pricey."

Comet bounded over to Deacon West.

Oh, shit.

"Comet, no!" Ross said a little too late.

The dog shoved his long snout into the man's crotch.

Ross let his eyes slide shut and waited for a lightning bolt to hit. When it didn't, he opened his eyes, took Comet by the collar, and said, "I'm so sorry. He's a rescue and not well mannered all the time. I'm working on it."

Deacon West actually blushed, and Ross couldn't blame him. Comet had just felt the poor guy up in front of several members of his congregation.

"Ms. Perez and I—" Ross had no idea how to make things right, "—we were wondering how you'd feel if I made the Nativity scene out of extra sheet metal I've got at my shop?" Not bad so far, even though he was totally winging it.

Deacon West's expression said he was skeptical. "Would it be tastefully done?"

Ross had no idea. He'd never made anything remotely close. "Sure." He rubbed the back of his neck. "Of course."

When every last one of their expressions brightened, Ross's confidence grew. "Would all the churches in Red River pitch in and paint it?" If he could drum up that much free paint, it would be a great way to make the church folks happy.

Deacon West and his followers all nodded. "I suppose so. What else can we do to help?"

Well, since they asked...

Deacon West was a leader in the community. Someone who could help heal the division in Red River that Ross and Kimberly had caused at the town council meeting. "Could you contact the other churches in town and try to get them on board with painting the Nativity scene?" Once Ross figured out how to make it. "And also with fulfilling some of the kids' wishes?" He rubbed the back of his neck, again. "This is about more than just decorations." At least it should've been, and Kimberly had been aware of that on a much deeper level than anyone else, himself included. "We want everyone in Red River to start working together. That's what our community is all about." He paused for effect. "That's what your faith is all about, too."

Deacon West pursed his lips. "Give us a minute." He turned to his group and they whispered. Then he turned back to Ross. "We're in." He hesitated. "We have a few requests, though."

The look on Deacon West's face said it wasn't really a request, but more like a command if Ross wanted their full support.

"I'm listening," Ross said.

"The Nativity scene *has* to be in good taste. We've seen some that included Santa and elves, and frankly, that just won't do. Especially since the rest of the town is usually decorating with the commercialized version of Christmas. Asking for this one thing to stay..." he seemed to be searching for the right words, "...traditional..." he then looked at his followers and they nodded, "...doesn't seem too much to ask in our opinion."

Ross nodded. "Agreed. You have my word I'll make the Nativity scene to your liking. What are your other requests?"

"How are the wishes for the gifts from the Wishing Tree going to be delivered?" Deacon West asked.

When they'd worked out their initial plan the night before at Kimberly's office, she'd mentioned hand delivering the gifts to the kids. It was the only way to ensure the presents arrived before Christmas so the kids wouldn't be disappointed. "I suppose we'll have to drive the gifts to each destination."

"We'd like the kids to be brought to Red River for an official ceremony on Christmas Eve." Deacon West beamed. "It'll demonstrate the true spirit of the season, which is giving and not receiving."

His followers nodded.

Ross had to agree on that point, but from what Kimberly had

said, the kids getting the wishes weren't just from Red River. She was collecting names from surrounding areas, too.

His gaze landed on each of Deacon West's group.

Their expressions said they were pretty proud of their idea.

Ross needed their support, so he blew out a sigh and gave them a nod. "Deal. Thank you for your help."

They said their goodbyes and waved as they left.

Now all he had to do was make a pattern for a baby in a manger, three kings bearing gifts, a virgin, and an archangel, and then cut life-sized figures of each out of scrap metal. Then figure out how to transport all the kids who were getting wishes to Red River. At the same time. For a ceremony that hadn't been scheduled yet, with Christmas just a few weeks away.

Piece of cake.

And snowballs wouldn't melt in hell.

CHAPTER EIGHT

Kimberly pulled up in front of *Ross's Automotive* to show him what she'd accomplished while she'd been on the road the past three days. It would've been nice to go home first to freshen up after driving all day, but when she'd texted him to let him know she was on her way back to Red River, he'd insisted she stop by his shop first.

She leaned forward to peer through the windshield at *aaaaaall* the lights. Holy cow, there were so many of them.

His shop and the lodge next door were both brighter than the sun, and twinkled like a supernova on steroids. She hadn't been to that end of Main Street since right after he'd put up his lights. He must've added more because both of his businesses were so lit they could probably be seen from Canada. Or outer space.

Ross really was a sap when it came to Christmas. He obviously had a good reason, though. Same way she had a great reason not to care about the season beyond what she could give out to kids who needed love.

Unable to maneuver the big moving truck into a parking spot, she shifted into first and parked perpendicular to the yellow lines, taking up several spaces. The gears made a grinding sound as she pressed the clutch and shifted again, barely able to reach the floorboard.

Geez. Because she was so short, driving a big truck with a standard transmission had been a challenge. Even with the seat pulled all the way forward, her legs were still too short to properly work the clutch. Never mind that she had to sit on a pillow to see over the steering wheel.

Ross would never let her live it down, so she killed the engine and hurried to climb out of the truck before anyone saw her. As she slammed the door, Ross strolled out of the reception area of Papa Bear's Lodge, carrying two thermal coffee mugs and already smiling as if he'd won the lottery.

Dang it.

There'd be no living around him now that he'd obviously seen her behind the wheel.

"I'm *back*." She tried to sound exasperated with him because of his incessant text messages telling her to get her ass back to Red River.

His nice fitting worn Levi's and insulated flannel shirt-jacket gave him enough of a bad-boy look to make her insides sigh, though, and she couldn't keep a stern look on her face. For a change, he wasn't wearing either a winter knit beanie or a ball cap. Instead, his hair looked freshly cut, and barely curled over the cuff of both ears.

Meow.

Get a grip. She steeled her resolve and put on a sassy face.

"Happy now? I came straight here, when I really wanted to go home for a shower."

The look on his face said he wasn't going to let a prime opportunity to tease her go after seeing her behind the wheel of a truck that was sized for a giant. "If you're expecting sympathy, you're going to be disappointed. Not after leaving me to deal with Ms. Clydelle by myself." He nodded to the truck. "You should've told me you'd be arriving in that thing. I'd have brought you a ladder."

He snorted with laughter. "Did you have to buy a booster seat to drive it?"

"No, I did not." Not exactly.

He held out a mug to her—the only reason she was glad she'd alerted him to her arrival—and let the bold roast roll down her throat.

He opened the door of the truck and doubled over laughing when he saw the pillows.

"Ha. Ha." She let a hand land on her hip. "I was lucky to find this truck for free. Beggars can't be choosey. Since we're on a budget consisting of less than zero dollars, I borrowed the truck from one of the organizations in Taos I've worked with to collect donations for families in need. One of them even delivered my car back to my office for me while I was driving this thing around the planet to pick up free decorations that are still worth a damn."

She shielded her eyes, as though it was high noon and the sun was blazing overhead, even though it was dark. "You should've told me you'd be decorating your businesses with enough lights to cause a sunburn. I'd have brought sunglasses." She snorted with laughter, mimicking him to perfection. "And sunscreen."

His irritation with her must've dialed down even more while they were apart, because he walked over and gently shoulder-checked her. "I've been busy, so you have a lot of catching up to do, smartass."

Smartass was a step up from Grinch, she'd give him that.

"I've come bearing gifts." A Grinch wouldn't do that. A smartass maybe, but not a Grinch. "We need to unload."

He held out an open palm. "Gimme the keys. I'll pull the truck into one of the bays. Go open the door for me. It's the big red button next to the far-left garage door." Once the keys were in his hand, he tossed them in the air and caught them again. "There's even fresh donuts waiting inside from the Ostergaards' bakery."

Well, that made not going home first for a shower worthwhile. There was nothing like fresh scones or pastries or donuts from the Ostergaards.

When she walked inside the garage, Comet bounded over to her. "Hey, you." She gave him a pat on the head. Of course, his master had made sure to put the Grinch antlers on the poor dog. He stayed at her side as she went to find the button, and she hooked a finger under his collar. "Can't have you darting in front of the truck, little buddy."

She opened the garage door, and Ross was already waiting to back the truck inside. To keep out the cold air, she closed the garage door as soon as the truck cleared the entrance. Once Ross turned off the engine, she let go of Comet's collar.

As Ross got out of the truck, she snatched the keys away and walked past him, then went around to the back of the truck to open the padlock. With a quick lift and twist of the lever, she swung open both doors and stepped aside, waving her arms across the content like a game show hostess.

"I collected as many donated hand-me-down decorations as possible from the companies I visited, *and* I was able to scavenge enough supplies to make the rest." She beamed at Ross, because heck yeah, she was pretty damned proud of herself. "Plus, those companies want to help fulfill the wishes for the kids." She cocked a hip and didn't miss the way Ross's eyes glazed over at the movement. It took him a second to refocus on her face.

On her *mouth*, actually.

Her heart skittered and skipped.

Which she ignored because it was the heated temperature inside the garage.

She pulled off her jacket and tossed it onto the bumper of the truck. "*And* I've set up an interview with the local newspaper to spread the word." She circled her arm in front of her, doing a victory dance. "I bet we'll end up with more donations than we have wishes, which means we can help even more kids." Excitement hummed through her. "I've already contacted more organizations so we can collect more wishes for the tree."

His eyes twinkled over the rim of his mug as he sipped.

"*Well?*" A little pat on the back would be nice. She'd driven around the world and back to accumulate nice decorations from companies who weren't going to use them anymore. Free of charge! "My idea to recycle decorations that still look brand new is freaking brilliant, isn't it?"

"I'm impressed." Ross angled his head and nodded, as though he really was dazzled by her cleverness. "I've come up with a few brilliant ideas myself while you left me here to answer to Ms. Clydelle's cane and Ms. Francine's purse." He shivered dramatically. "Thank God they didn't break out the scary gavel."

Kimberly pretended to act coy. "I *am* sorry about that part, but..." She did her gameshow hostess routine again. "Problems solved. This is all we need to decorate the entire town and finish the tree. That should get everyone, including the two elderly sisters wielding the purse and cane like weapons, off our backs."

His lips thinned.

"*Yeeeeaaah*, not exactly." He scrubbed a palm over his stubbled jaw.

Oh, no.

He kept rubbing one cheek. "My attempt to keep everyone in Red River happy—and it was a valiant attempt, mind you—"

"What have you done?" She did not want to know. Not really.

"While you were gone, I made a giant Nativity scene from scrap metal." He frowned. "I can't say it's a fantastic likeness of the baby Jesus, but I did my best. I even put it up in the park this morning, just to see how it looks." He shrugged. "I think it'll do, especially on such short notice. Tomorrow, I'll take it down and deliver the pieces to Deacon West. He's got every church in town lined up to paint it."

Kimberly's head snapped back. "That *is* brilliant." She started her victory be-bopping to imaginary music again, thrilled at their progress. "No worries, then. With the lights you collected locally and everything else I scavenged, we've got plenty for the tree, every street lamp in town, and the gazebo." She hooked a thumb at the truck. "I started making the ornaments while I was on the road. They'll be in the shape of snowflakes, with a wish written on each one. I've got the supplies we need to finish them. It'll be a snap."

The jaw rubbing didn't stop, and he wouldn't meet her gaze.

Her boogie-woogie came to an abrupt halt. "Stop prolonging the agony, and just tell me."

He folded both arms and stared at the ground. "I know you planned to deliver the gifts to the kids around the area—"

"Try around the whole state. I've already got several lists sitting in my inbox with hundreds of names on them." Kimberly's stomach started to tighten. She had a feeling she wasn't going to like what Ross was about to say.

"Yeah, about that..."

Oh, hells bells. Now she *knew* she wasn't going to like whatever it was he was going to tell her.

"I sort of made a commitment to the church folks..." he stuffed both hands in his pockets, "...that the kids would all come to Red River and open the gifts here on Christmas Eve."

Her jaw went slack. "Ross!" she blurted when she finally recovered. "How are we going to get that many kids to Red River?"

He held up a hand. "Got it covered. I called one of my wealthy out-of-state clients who sends me his classic cars for repairs. He owns a tour bus company, and he's agreed to send us as many as we need. A fleet, even."

Kimberly put both hands on her cheeks. "There will need to be some sort of organized welcome committee and food to feed the kids. I don't know if we have the money for all that."

Ross's expression blanked. Obviously, he hadn't thought through the details.

"And they'll need a place to stay overnight because they can't go all the way back home the same night if they're coming from all over the state." She paced. "Chaperones!" She whirled around. "We'll need chaperones, too." She dropped her head into her hands. "How are we going to get all this done in time?"

"Fuck's sake." Ross ran his fingers through his hair. "I didn't realize what all would go into it. I'm sorry."

"Well, bless your big heart." Kimberly kept pacing. Anybody from a small town like Red River knew that was a polite way of saying "what the hell were you thinking?"

"It's going to work out, and it'll be great for the kids." He walked to the counter and threw a treat into Comet's dog bed. The dog curled up in the bed and went to work on the chewy strip that resembled a piece of bacon.

Kimberly tapped her foot, folding her arms over her chest.

Then Ross picked up a big white box. "I promise we'll figure it out," he said when he joined her.

"*We?*" She raised both brows. "I didn't create this mess."

He screwed up his face. "You kinda did when you went to the town council meeting and tried to have Christmas canceled."

She scoffed and threw her hands in the air because he was twisting the truth just to needle her.

He waggled both brows, then threw down the gauntlet. "So, are you gonna whine about it or are you gonna boss up?" He opened the box, the scent of powdered sugar and warm cream filled donuts made her eyes slide shut.

When she opened them again, the shrewd glint in his eyes told her he thought he'd won that round.

She leveled a tight smile at him. "First of all, I'm 'a do both." She let her gaze drop to the luscious desserts. "Second of all..." She snatched the whole box. "I'm gonna eat every last one of these without sharing with the likes of you."

His smile widened. "You do that." He went to a small round table in the back corner of the garage and pulled out a chair for her. "Have a seat and give me the blow by blow details of your awesomeness on the road."

When she sat, he claimed the other chair, pulling it closer, and leaned in so their knees brushed.

A tingle started at her lips, where his stare kept anchoring, and traveled down her arms, her legs, settling in her...

She clenched from the waist down.

"You look nice, by the way." He inched closer.

She looked down at her outfit, and whatdya know? Her clothes matched again. She'd brought nicer than usual outfits on her trip to make a good impression at the companies she'd approached.

"I like this new look on you, although your regular wardrobe works just as well." His green eyes darkened. "Your usual clothes probably wouldn't look so good on anyone else, but it's just so ... you."

She was pretty sure that was a compliment. The spark in his eyes was definitely more than friendly admiration.

And that just wouldn't do.

She pulled off her winter knit cap and ran her fingers through her short hair, making it stand on end.

When the lusty glint in his eyes only deepened, she speared her hair again and tousled it for good measure.

There. That should do it. There wasn't a man on the planet she hadn't been able to scare away with her wild hair.

Except for Ross Armstrong, apparently.

His gaze dropped to her mouth, causing her breath to catch.

A shiver skated over her.

So she took an obnoxious bite of a cream-filled donut that was covered in thick powdered sugar. The kind of messy, sloppy bite that used to piss off any one of her foster parents who were getting too touchy or only wanted her in the house for the paycheck, which they spent on a cable shopping network or on lottery tickets.

But...

Oh, my gawd. The donut was so divine. And still warm.

Her eyes slid shut and she chewed. Her taste buds ignited like a fireworks show as the scrumptious flavor melted on her tongue. "*Mmmm. So good.*"

Ross's knees moved to frame hers, and her eyes snapped open.

The hunger in his gaze was pure fire and passion.

The desire in her heart was pure fear and panic.

He was just too good of a guy.

He was just too irresistible.

Nope. Nope. Nopity nope.

She put down the donut to wipe her hands and leave before she did something at least one of them would end up regretting.

Before she could get up, he cupped her jaw, putting a finger under her chin to gently make her look at him. His gaze hooked into hers and she knew she was a goner. "Don't run away this time."

She opened her mouth to say *no, she had to go*. Like right then, before her bra flew open on its own and her panties melted off just from the yearning in his expression. Instead, she said, "'M'kay," in the meekest voice that didn't sound anything like her usual spunky tone.

She tried to wiggle farther away, but her chair butted up against the wall.

"I've cared about you for a long time, Kimberly, but you shut me out just when our relationship started to get interesting." One corner of his mouth curved a fraction. "Actually, my relationship with you has been interesting since day one, but you know what I mean."

"I..." She tried to look away, but the soft touch of his fingers brought her gaze back to his. "I don't do relationships, Ross. I'm not very good at them, and I care enough about you to *not* want to put you through that kind of personal hell."

He shook his head, smoothing a thumb across her cheek. "That's not all of it. It's not only me you're trying to protect. It's you, too."

She stiffened, because how dare he?

"I know what I'm talking about. My parents are the same way." His hand moved upward, his fingers flexing against her flesh to stroke and caress.

Heat ignited at her core, spiraling outward until it singed her fingertips and curled her toes. Her hands obviously had a mind of their own, because they slipped under his jacket and pressed flat against his thermal shirt. His muscled chest tensed and rolled under her touch.

"I'm so sorry you lost someone you loved," she whispered. "It must've been painful."

"It was." He nodded. "But life goes on for the living. My sister asked me and my parents to make the most of every Christmas as a way to keep her memory alive. My folks haven't exactly lived up to their end of the bargain."

He didn't offer up details, Instead, he drew in a deep breath and let it out again. The warmth of it caressed over Kimberly's face and neck, and she moved her fingertips in small, soft circles against his chest.

"If you grew up in foster care, then you've lost people you loved, too." His eyes filled with compassion.

That was Kimberly's undoing because most people responded to her upbringing with pity. Pity was a four-letter curse word that she couldn't tolerate.

Pity could go fuck itself.

She would never be a victim of her past, and that's why she'd worked so hard to get through college and law school. So she could use her education and brains to help other kids who had difficult lives and unfortunate circumstances that were no fault of their own.

She nodded, a sting starting behind her eyes.

Oh, dear God, no.

She did not, under any circumstances, cry in front of other people. It didn't take long in the system for kids to learn not to show emotion, especially not tears. Tears were a sign of weakness that could be exploited.

"Who did you lose, Kimberly?" Ross's voice was so soft and so loving that the sting behind her eyes turned to wetness that threatened to spill over. "Are your parents still living?"

That chipped away the last of her resolve and the dam broke, tears streaming down her face. "No." She swiped at her cheek. "They left me alone in our apartment. It wasn't that unusual when they were on a drug bender, even though I was still pretty young, but that time they didn't come back for days. Finally, I went to a convenience store down

the street because I was so hungry and there was no food at home."
She drew in a hiccupy breath from crying. "I was caught shoplifting,
and that's when the authorities put me in foster care. My parents
knew because the police found them strung out in some crack house,
sobered them up, and told them what had happened to me."

She let out a throaty, moaning cry from deep in her soul. A
place she'd kept locked up so tight she'd thought it had died long
ago. Maybe it had just been hidden all that time. Hidden behind
snarky comments and witty comebacks. Hidden underneath wild
hair and ostentatious clothes.

He gathered her up in his strong arms and placed her in his lap,
stroking her back and her hair while she let out the deep well of
emotions that she'd been pretending for years didn't exist.

"Let it out, babe," he whispered. "I've got you."

When her fit of tears subsided, she sniffled into his shoulder.
"They never came back for me."

She'd told herself for years they'd probably overdosed in a crack
house just like the one the police had found them at while she'd sat
in the back seat of a police car for stealing a bag of potato chips.
While she'd sat in one foster home after another, waiting for them
to wise the hell up and come get her so they could be the family
they were meant to be.

They never did.

"When I was in law school, me and Angelique did some checking. They were both gone." As she'd expected, her mom really had
OD'd. Her father had passed away in the hospital because of
complications brought on by years of drug and alcohol abuse.

Even if they'd still been living, they wouldn't have deserved her
forgiveness or her compassion. At least that's what she'd told
herself to survive, instead of hanging on to false hope that
would've only served to make her relive the pain and rejection over
and over again.

So why did her heart feel like it was breaking in two because of
loneliness for the parents who hadn't given a rat's ass about her?

He framed her face with his hands and leaned back to stare into her eyes. "You know me pretty well by now. Do you think I'd ever let you down?"

She wanted to say she wasn't sure, but deep down, she knew that wasn't true. He was a stand up guy, and anyone who crossed paths with Ross Armstrong knew it.

She shook her head. "No, I don't think you would."

His eyes softened, pinning her with a look that said his feelings for her went way beyond friendship. And for the first time, that didn't send her running for the door.

"Then give me a chance." He placed a soft kiss on the corner of her mouth. "Give *us* a chance." He pressed another sweet kiss on the other corner of her mouth, then grazed her lips with his. "I've wished for this for so long."

Need lanced through her.

One of his hands slipped under her top to massage circles up her spine while the other dropped to her neck, the roughness of his palm causing her skin to prickle, and she shivered.

"Are you cold?" he whispered against her mouth.

She shook her head. "No."

The twinkle that said he was both happy and victorious was back, and he chuckled. "Then you want me as much as I want you."

One arm circled his neck. The other played with the strands of his sandy blond hair that brushed the rim of his ear. "Maybe."

He pressed a kiss to her neck. "You can't resist busting my chops, can you?"

"Uh-uh." She traced a fingertip over the cuff of his ear all the way to his earlobe and along his squared jaw.

The rich timbre of his growl against her ear—so masculine, so sexy—made her feel so wanted. Not something she was used to, and she found it irresistible.

So irresistible, in fact, that she crushed her lips to his and speared her fingers into his hair. His hungry kiss consumed her.

Sent a current of electricity coursing through her to settle in her nipples.

Before she knew what was happening, he shifted her so she straddled him.

She pressed her aching nipples against him, and he groaned again. "Too many—"

She cut him off with another hot open-mouth kiss.

"—clothes," he said, shucking his jacket. Then he went in for more, but before he could slip his muscled arms around her again, she tugged at the hem of his thermal shirt.

"Great idea." He reached behind his head and one-handed his shirt to send it sailing across the table.

"I'm full of great ideas." She ran open palms up his bare arms and ground her hips against his.

"*Jesus,*" Ross hissed, placing one hand at the back of her head and the other at the small of her back to pull her as close as possible, then he kissed the hell out of her.

Fine by her.

She sighed into his kiss, a shiver quaking through her as one of his hands slid under her black turtleneck to smooth up her bare back.

She leaned away, giving him a melodramatic sensual look. "If you think it's been good so far..." She fingered the hem of her sweater and tugged it off in one smooth movement.

Thank goodness she'd worn a nice bra.

His eyes darkened with desire. "Black lace." His voice had gone thick and rough.

"It's new. I don't usually spend money on such things, but I treated myself while I was on the road." As his gaze roamed over her, she straightened her spine, letting him take his fill of her enormous rack.

His stare snagged on her belly button. "You're pierced," he rasped out.

"Yup." Gently, she took his hands in hers and placed them over her breasts.

He cupped and kneaded, making her head fall back and her eyes slide shut.

Making the space between her thighs go moist.

She circled her hips against his.

"*Holy shit,*" he hissed out, and reached to her back to unhook her bra.

Both breasts sprang free, nipples hardened into peaks, and waiting for his touch.

"Good Lord, woman." His gaze turned sultry as he filled his palms with her aching flesh. "I've never seen anything as beautiful as you." His warm mouth closed over a nipple, and she cried out, wrapping both arms around his head.

He suckled until every nerve ending in her body threatened to spontaneously combust. She rocked her hips into his, finding a perfect rhythm that drove her close to the edge, even with their pants still on.

She leaned back to go for his zipper.

The door slammed open, and Dylan McCoy charged in.

Comet sprang to life and barked at the intruder.

Kimberly scrambled off of Ross's lap and turned away to find her top.

"*Shit,*" Ross hissed under his breath and reached for his shirt.

"Uh." Dylan averted his gaze. "Sorry, guys, but the door wasn't locked. You better come quick."

That was exactly what Kimberly had been trying to do until he so rudely interrupted! She pulled on her shirt and spun to face him. "Why?"

Dylan still kept his gaze facing the wall. "Chairperson Clydelle came into Cotton Eyed Joe's pretty frantic and sent me to get you."

"What's so important?" Ross asked, still trying to turn his shirt inside out.

Kimberly gawked at him like a woman lusting after a male bare-all calendar.

His bare chest glistened with a fine sheen of dew from getting hot and bothered. Because of her hip grinding. Because of her bare breasts. Because of the fact he cared about her and had been about to show her how much.

Kimberly's mouth watered at the sight of him, and she couldn't help but lick her lips.

He glanced up and did a double take, their eyes anchoring to each other. Time slowed, everything around them melted away, and it was just him and her and the unrequited feelings and physical attraction that had almost *not* been so unrequited anymore.

So close.

Dylan cleared his throat.

Both Ross and Kimberly's heads snapped around.

"Um, sorry," Kimberly mumbled, heat prickling up her neck to settle in her cheeks.

"Yeah, uh, right…" Ross fumbled over his words as much as he was fumbling to right his shirt. "Sorry, but not really, uh…"

Kimberly doubled over laughing.

Which caused Ross to do the same, because that was the beauty of their friendship. The beauty of *them*.

Her heart skipped a beat at the realization that she'd finally thought of *them* as a beautiful thing. Or at least the beginning of something beautiful.

Dylan let out an exasperated sigh, and Ross and Kimberly's laughter trailed off into silence. They gave Dylan their full attention.

"Finished now?" Dylan asked with a smartass tone.

Ross glanced at her and shook his head. "No. Not by a long shot, but you're here, so go ahead and tell us what's wrong." He pulled his shirt over his head and stood.

"There's practically a riot going on over in the park," Dylan said.

Ross's brow wrinkled. "What?"

"*Why?*" Kimberly gasped.

Dylan volleyed a look between the two of them. "Something to do with the decorations and the tree."

Oh, for crying out loud.

Kimberly went for her jacket. "Who started this nonsense?"

"That's what I'd like to know." Ross pulled on his jacket, too.

"Don't know." Dylan shook his head. "But Ms. Clydelle said you two better get to the park because it was your job to sort it out and fix it."

CHAPTER NINE

Ross pulled his classic pickup along the curb in front of the park and propped an elbow on the door.

Fuck's sake.

"Oh, no," Kimberly said from the passenger's seat.

He tapped a fist against his chin and watched the mob that had gathered in the park. They'd clearly squared off into two opposing groups.

His scrap iron Nativity figures had been spray painted by vandals before he could take them down and deliver them to Deacon West to be painted the right way. The three wise men were painted to look like elves, the archangel, Gabriel, resembled Santa Claus, the Virgin Mary had been painted to look like Mrs. Claus ... in a mini-dress.

Ross could see why that had the churchgoers in an uproar.

Kimberly gasped, her hands flying to her cheeks. "Look at the tree."

Ross's gazed scanned the park, landing on the eye soar that used to be the Wishing Tree. Just above the mob's head, the branches had been visibly sheared off, in the shape of a...

Ross pinched the corners of his eyes with a thumb and forefinger. "I swear that wasn't my doing."

"What kind of people clip a Grinch shape into a Christmas tree that's meant to help kids?" Kimberly huffed.

Good question. He damn well would have an answer, too, by the time he was done diffusing the situation. He was already in a grouchy mood because he and Kimberly were interrupted at the worst possible moment. But being interrupted for this?

Now he knew what the bumper stickers *Random Bitch Moment Waiting to Happen* meant because he was about to have one. Maybe he could order a sticker for his truck that said *bastard,* instead. Either way, he was pissed that people could be so immature and thoughtless. The fact they were acting so selfish at this time of year only made Ross's mood more pissy.

"Come on." He opened his door, got out, and slammed it hard.

Kimberly hopped out and obviously remembered to let Comet out of the back seat because they both hurried to catch up to him.

He didn't slow his gait. Didn't soften his scowl.

He walked right up to the crowd. "Who the hell is responsible for this?" he barked.

The crowd went quiet.

"Someone better start talking." He rammed his hands into his jacket pockets.

Finally, Deacon West stepped forward. "You promised us a tasteful Nativity scene." He pointed to the iron figures. "The crude welding was excusable under the circumstances, but this is insulting."

What Ross hadn't been able to see from his truck was that someone had adorned Baby Jesus with a costume so that He looked like an Elf on the Shelf.

For the love of God.

So, so, literally, too.

Ross had grown up in church, but his parents had stopped going after they lost Noelle. Still, vandalizing any faith seemed wrong, especially at Christmastime.

A middle-aged woman with bushy shoulder length hair spoke

to Deacon West. "So you retaliated by ruining the tree?" She pointed to the Grinch silhouette cut into the giant pine.

Deacon West's expression said he was truly incensed. "We did no such thing. I don't know who ruined the tree, but it wasn't us, I assure you."

An argument broke out with lots of sneers and jeers coming from both sides.

Ross was about to lose his shit, so he laced his fingers behind his head and closed his eyes for a second. Then he opened them and scanned the crowd. Two small groups of middle-school aged kids lingered in the background on both sides—one set of tweens behind the churchgoers, and the other set of tweens behind the tree-lovers.

Ross would bet money he had his vandals.

He didn't know anything about parenting, except that kids usually mimicked their parents' behavior.

He glanced around the crowd of adults behaving badly. Seriously, some Hollywood producer could make a mint if they filmed the scene for a reality TV show.

When the melee didn't subside, Ross crouched, molded two big handfuls of snow into balls, and stood with one in each hand.

Kimberly stepped up beside him. "Need help, big guy?"

He handed her one of the snowballs. "I'll take one group. You take the other."

Her big smile was full of mischief.

"On three?"

"You got it, big guy." Kimberly zeroed in on her target.

So did he. "One." Ross started the countdown. "Two." They reared back their throwing arms for the pitch. "Three." They let the snowballs fly, shocking the entire crowd into silence.

When they had everyone's attention, Ross said, "Listen up, because I'm only going to say this once."

He glanced at Kimberly and did a double take. Her big eyes looked up at him with so much lust and admiration that he couldn't make himself look away.

He lost his train of thought for a second.

She waggled her fingers toward the dumbstruck crowd. "Carry on while you've got their attention."

He cleared his throat and refocused on the crowd. "I don't know who did this or why, but Kimberly and I have been working our tails off trying to make everyone in this town happy, and this is the thanks we get?" For the life of him, he couldn't get the son-of-a-bitch tone back into his voice because all he could think about was the sight of Kimberly's lustful expression.

She went on tiptoes and said in his ear, "Come on, you've got 'em on the ropes. Don't let them off the hook yet."

He glanced at the vandalized Nativity scene and the ruined tree and the fury was back again. "I've never been more disappointed in this town than I am at this moment, so here's how it's gonna go down." He drew himself up and jutted out his chest. He was well over six feet tall, and when he puffed up, he knew how intimidating he could be. "Deacon West, tell your congregation ... and all the other congregations in town—" Couldn't hurt to throw down the guilt card on all of them at the same time. "—to start acting out their faith instead of just talking about it."

Deacon West nodded absently, as though he was shocked at Ross's hardass tone.

"I'll expect each church in town to provide a *live* Nativity scene every night, starting when we officially light the Wishing Tree." He craned his neck, searching for the kids on the churchgoers side, who were likely either youth group members or their parents were active members of one of the churches in Red River. "And that includes the kids here tonight."

Every last one of the teens and tweens huddling on the fringe of the crowd blanched.

Good. He hadn't met a kid that age yet who couldn't use a good kick in the pants at least once before they reached adulthood. He'd been one of them himself at one time, acting out after the loss of his sister because of the pent-up grief he wasn't allowed to talk about because of his parents' selfish denial.

Kimberly leaned into him. "Clever idea."

Maybe, but he was too damn angry to give himself any credit.

He focused on the opposing side of the mob. "And you all can organize carolers to sing holiday songs in the park, rotating out every night, just like the Nativity scene will do." He searched the crowd again, finding the kids who were likely responsible for vandalizing the baby Jesus and His scrap iron posse. The way they kicked the dirt and shot terrified looks at each other told Ross he wasn't wrong. "The kids here tonight *will* help out with that, too."

He let his gaze bounce around the crowd. "I'm going to find a new tree first thing tomorrow, and it'll be decorated and ready to light by this weekend." With everything else he and Kimberly had to accomplish before Christmas Eve, it would be tight, but he'd either get the new tree ready, or die trying. "Both sides better not fail to perform their responsibilities, or else..."

What? *What* else could be sure to make both sides suffer the consequences of their ridiculous behavior?

He had nothin'.

Ruining Christmas ... acting the Grinch, just wasn't him, no matter how angry he was.

"Or else, tomorrow we'll decorate Red River with Valentine's decorations and have you dress up like leprechauns and Easter bunnies instead of Christmas carolers and a Nativity scene," Kimberly finished for him.

Both sides of the mob gasped.

Comet barked.

Ross looked down at her and mouthed, "Thank you."

She shrugged. "Sometimes being a Grinch comes in handy."

Sure as hell did.

He turned his attention back to the stunned mob. "Any questions?" He didn't wait for an answer. "Good. Be ready this weekend to sing your hearts out and reenact a two-thousand-year-old stable scene in Bethlehem." He paused for dramatic effect. "Or you can expect a lot of red hearts and green four-leaf clovers in Red River this year. I doubt the kids getting their wishes fulfilled will care one way or the other, folks, as long as our town is bright and sparkly."

Now, who was the Grinch? Because he'd just managed to stomp all over his sister's dying wish by threatening to deprive Red River of the correct holiday decorations.

He took Kimberly by the arm. "Come on, let's go."

Before he could start toward the truck, something tugged at his pants leg. He looked down, and a little girl bundled in winter gear and clutching a teddy bear had her bottom lip puckered out so far it could've caught snowflakes if it had been snowing. She couldn't have been more than four or five.

"Mister," she pouted. "Will Santa skip Red River if we don't have Christmas lights? He won't be able to find us."

Her mother shot out of the crowd. "I'm so sorry." She tried to lead the little girl away.

"Ma'am." Ross couldn't be a Grinch to a kid with a pout as cute as the one this little girl had. "May I?" He held out his hands in a gesture that said he wanted to pick her up.

The young mother nodded.

When Ross had her in his arms, he asked, "What's your name?"

"Noelle." Her little voice and pouting lip made it sound more like *Know-ewwwl*.

Sadness reached up and grabbed him by the throat. Wouldn't let go. Wouldn't let him speak.

"She was born in December," the little girl's mother explained.

Kimberly's hand slipped under his jacket, and she flattened it against the small of his back in a comforting gesture. "I've got this."

Thank God, because Ross couldn't have spoken a word without blubbering like an idiot.

She tweaked the little girl's nose. "Sweetie, I can already tell you're going to be at the top of Santa's Nice List."

Noelle's face lit brighter than the lights strung around both of Ross's businesses.

Kimberly had given Ross just enough time to compose himself.

Ish. "I'll put in a good word for you with Santa." The croakiness in his voice was barely noticeable.

"Really?" Noelle asked, but it came out more like "Weawwy?"

"Of course. How could a kiddo as sweet as you *not* be the first rooftop Santa lands on this year?" That time, Kimberly tweaked Noelle's cheek. "So make sure you leave an extra cookie and a biggie size glass of milk, because I bet he spends a lot of time at your house unloading gifts and filling your stocking."

Noelle's mom beamed and nodded.

Noelle's lip jutted out again, as though she wasn't convinced. "But last year he skipped my house." Tears welled in her eyes. "My other mommy said we didn't have any lights up, so he couldn't find us."

Ross and Kimberly glanced at each other, then at Noelle's mom. She took the little girl from Ross and set her down. "Hon, can you go play on the swings for a second?" She pointed to the swing sets across the park.

When Noelle scampered away, her mom said, "I'm her foster mom. When the social worker gave me her birthdate, I assumed that's why she was named Noelle." Her gaze kept darting toward the little girl, apparently not wanting to let Noelle out of her sight. "Her last foster home was..." She glanced away, obviously unsure of what to say. "Well, she was neglected. A friend of mine works in Child and Family Services for the state. She asked me and my husband if we'd take Noelle on a temporary basis until they find a responsible foster home." She eyed Noelle affectionately. "Or a nice family to adopt her."

"*If...*" Kimberly interrupted. Splayed fingers went to rest just under her collarbone. "*If* they find a family to adopt her."

The heartbreak in Kimberly's expression was palpable. It tore Ross's thudding heart right out of his chest.

The crowd started to disperse.

"Right." Noelle's mom seemed a little embarrassed. "My husband and I own the Rocket Pizza Parlor here in town. We're in the process of opening three more in different vacation towns throughout the Rockies." Her gaze dropped to the ground. "I just found out I'm pregnant, and I don't think I can handle all of the changes at once, so we're hoping an adoptive family will come along and fall in love with her. She's a great kid, but—"

Kimberly held up her hand. "You don't owe anyone an explanation, least of all us." The professional attorney, who obviously had a lot of experience in family court, surfaced. "You can only do so much, and it's better you know your limitations up front than to take on something you can't handle." She paused. Drew in a stream of air, then let it rush out again. "Or something you can't finish." Her voice went a little shaky on the last sentence.

"Well, thank you for saying such sweet things to her." Noelle's foster mom let her stare slide to the swing set where the little girl swung back and forth, singing *Frosty the Snowman* loud enough to carry across the park.

Her off-key child's voice made Ross's chest squeeze so tight he could barely breathe.

"I'll try to make sure she gets enough gifts to make up for the years she had to do without," said her foster mom.

"Let us know if you need help with that." Kimberly's voice was ragged with emotion. "We can add her to the Wishing Tree if you need us to. That's what it's for."

"Thank you," said the young woman. She went to get Noelle and led her out of the park.

Kimberly's silence and the wetness shimmering in her eyes said she was as choked up as he was.

"Hey." He put an arm around her waist and pulled her flush against him. "Noelle is going to be fine. She's in a good home."

Kimberly gave her head a quick shake. "For now—" Her voice cracked.

"Tell me what it was like." His grip around her waist tightened. "I'm here, and I'm not going anywhere."

The crowd thinned as everyone left in different directions.

A tear slid down her cheek, and she swiped at it. "One of my foster parents used to house at least four kids at a time. We'd have to eat soup out of a can every day because she said she couldn't afford the gas it would cost to heat it on the stove. She used all the money she got for us to buy scratch-off lottery tickets." Another tear streamed. "When Christmas rolled around, there were no gifts." Kimberly eased out of his grasp. "She said Santa didn't visit poor kids."

Scalding anger pounded through his veins. How could people be so cruel? "Oh, babe. I'm so sorry."

She took another sidestep away from him. "I'm sorry, too, Ross, but I can't do this. I don't have anything to offer you." The street lamps in the park glinted off the wet streaks on her cheeks. "There is *nothing* left inside of me to give." She pointed toward the direction Noelle and her foster mom had left. "They just reminded me of that, and better that they did, because I need to take my own advice." She took another step, distancing herself from him. "I can't let us start something one of us won't be able to finish."

He took a step toward her and opened his arms. "Babe, don't—"

She darted out of his reach. "Don't call me that. I'm nobody's babe and never will be." She turned and set out in a dead run across the park in the direction of her office.

He scrubbed a hand over his jaw and stared after her. He had no idea how much time passed, but finally, he turned to head toward his truck and pulled up short when Chairperson Clydelle's cane poked him in the chest.

"That's your way of fixing things?" she groused.

Ms. Francine was at her side. Purse dangling. Tongue tisking.

Comet whined.

Ross knew exactly how the poor dog felt.

"Leprechauns and Valentine's hearts? And now your partner in crime has run off to God knows where again?" Ms. Clydelle waved the cane in Kimberly's direction. "Fix this, or you'll wish you'd never grown up in Red River."

As much as Ross hated to admit he'd been bested by two little old ladies, he believed her.

CHAPTER TEN

Kimberly paced the length of her office.

Her heart wasn't just thundering against her chest from running all the way from the park. No, it was hammering against her ribcage because of little Noelle. Because of the years of neglect Kimberly had suffered. Because of the memories of never knowing when her time would be up at one home and what circumstances the next would offer.

The few times she'd moved to a nice, normal home, it hadn't lasted long *because* it had been a nice, normal home with nice, normal parents who didn't know how to handle a messed-up kid like her.

By the time she aged out of the foster system, she'd known she would never be nice and normal. She'd never have nice and normal to offer anyone.

She trekked back to her desk and snatched up her phone. Her hands trembled as she typed a text message to Ross. They had a solid plan in place to get Red River ready for the holidays. He could handle his share of the responsibilities and she could handle hers without working side by side. When they did need to spend time together, she'd make sure they weren't alone.

The sound of someone crashing through the front door made Kimberly freeze. Then the door slammed shut again.

Ross appeared in the doorway, breathing heavily, as though he'd run to her office from the park, too. He braced a hand against the doorframe as Comet appeared at his side, panting.

The look of determination in his eyes made her swallow back sheer terror. Terror that she'd cave in unless she could get him to leave first. Terror that he'd see how empty, how desolate she really was on the inside if their relationship went any further or any deeper than just friendship.

"Ross, I can't—"

"Yes, you can." He pushed off the doorframe and came toward her with measured, fluid steps.

"You don't understand." She backed up until her butt came up against the desk.

"Maybe I don't, Kimberly." He kept coming at her until he was a breath away. "You don't understand what I went through losing my sister, either."

She pointed to her phone. "Um, I was just sending you a text about what happened in the park and what we can do about it." Changing the subject back to the mob in the park seemed like the best idea. Focusing on work had always helped keep her mind off of her pathetic life.

Off of her pathetic self.

"You know we can't leave the Nativity scene and the caroling up to them. Not after what they've done," she said. "We have to keep after them."

He took the phone from her hands and tossed it onto the desk. "I don't care about that right now. We'll deal with them later." He braced a hand on each side of her, hemming her in, as though he was trying to keep her from escaping. "Right now, all I care about is you. We're going to deal with *us*."

"Ross." Her words were a plea. "There is no us."

"Exactly." His gaze raked her face. "But there should be. There is no reason for there not to be an us."

"Yes, there is," she protested.

"No, there's not," he countered.

She let her head fall back and her eyes slide shut.

"Kimberly, look at me."

The way he said her name made a shiver of longing race over her. She opened her eyes.

His heated breaths washed over her, and he brushed his nose against hers. "I keep telling you that you can count on me."

That was the problem. Ross was the most solid person Kimberly knew, and he deserved someone who wasn't emotionally crippled.

Her lips parted, but she couldn't speak.

He was such a lovely man. She couldn't say yes, but she sure as hell couldn't bring herself to say no, either.

He must've sensed her resignation, because he placed a kiss where her neck met her shoulder, then dragged his nose all the way up to her ear to nibble on the lobe.

A shudder of desire raced through her, and she flattened both palms against his chest as she gave in to the attraction, the connection between them she could no longer deny.

He nuzzled her ear, his warm, wet breaths making her body react so violently that she was almost convulsing.

"This," he whispered. "*This* is the way it's supposed to be between us." One hand dropped to the back of her thigh, and he lifted her leg to wrap it around his waist. "You have no idea how long I've wanted this. How long I've waited for this." His voice turned to a growl. "How long I've wished for this."

That was her undoing. She'd secretly wished to be with Ross for so very, very long. Wished that she was the type of person who could let go and trust. Ross was the only man who'd managed to get her to consider it, even slightly.

Her hands slid up to his shoulders, then into his hair. "Should I put your wish on the tree?"

"Not necessary anymore." His hands grabbed her ass cheeks, and he scooped her up in one quick movement.

She squeaked and wrapped both legs around him.

"It's coming true right here, right now." He took her mouth in a punishing kiss and walked to the sofa.

She didn't unwrap her legs from him as he laid her down, pulling him along to cover her body with his. He ground his hips into her center, and she arched into him as his rock-hard shaft pulsed against her.

An electric current of sexual desire lit every nerve, every cell on fire.

Good Lord, if he could make her feel like she was about to spontaneously combust fully clothed, she couldn't imagine what it would be like when he finally did enter the Promised Land.

She pulled at his clothes.

He shucked his jacket and shirt and came down on top of her again, devouring her neck with his mouth, teeth, and tongue.

Comet whined, and she broke the kiss.

"Comet," Ross grumbled and pointed to the door. "Go."

Surprisingly, Comet obeyed and trotted to the doorway.

"Stay," Ross said, looking over his shoulder at the dog.

She framed his faced with both of her hands and pulled his mouth back to hers. Her kiss was frantic and frenzied, as she let her fear seep away and opened her heart. She wanted him. Every part of him. Protecting him by staying emotionally and physically distant wasn't an option anymore because he'd chipped away the last of her resolve.

She broke the kiss and stared into his eyes. Got lost for a moment, then made herself refocus. She molded a palm to his cheek, gently. Lovingly. "I keep telling *you*," she mimicked his words from earlier. "I'm not good at long term." Long-term relationships. Long-term feelings or emotions.

Because nothing lasts forever, even when people promise that something will.

So giving him an out seemed only fair, but she found herself hoping he wouldn't take it. Found herself holding her breath, wanting him to say she was worth the risk, because no one in her life had ever told her so.

The emotions shimmering in his eyes that said he wasn't taking the easy way out, no matter how many times she offered it, made her heart shatter. Then the same glittering desire, need, and tenderness put her heart back together again, one sliver at a time until she couldn't breathe.

"There's a first time for everything." His head dipped, and he pressed a kiss behind her ear.

She quivered.

"We're both flawed." His kisses grew hungrier as he trailed them along her jawline. "Together, though, we might be perfectly imperfect."

Her heart stuttered. Oh, my *gawd*. Was that the sexiest thing she'd ever heard or what?

He swallowed her sigh with a deep, desperate kiss.

Flames of lust engulfed her, and she was lost in his touch as his hands traveled over her. He sat up, and she went for the button on his jeans. Before she could unzip them, he covered her hands with his. Took one of her hands and helped her stand.

He kicked off his boots and socks and laid back against the sofa, shirtless. Jeans unbuttoned. Hands laced behind his head and ankles crossed. And then he just stared at her with a lazy smile on his lips.

"What?" She gave him a frown.

He didn't answer with words. Instead, he let one brow arch high, and his gaze traveled down her length, then up again.

"You want me to strip?" Her jaw fell open, dramatically.

One of his shoulders lifted. "Call it another wish."

Her hands went to her hips. "More like a fantasy."

He angled his head in a *you got me there* look. "Fantasy works for me. Either way, I finally get to see you *completely* naked, and I want to savor it."

The look of pure lust in his eyes made her breath hitch. If it was a show he wanted, then it was a show he was going to get.

She fingered the hem of her top. When she slowly lifted it, his gaze hung on the small gold ring at her belly button, just as it had in his garage.

His eyes grew smoky with desire.

"It was a college-girl whim," she explained.

"I suddenly find myself a huge fan of college-girl whims." He actually licked his lips as he kept staring at her piercing. "I'm going to need to examine that one closely. With my tongue."

Heat licked over her skin as his gaze found hers again. She tossed her top aside. When she was down to her panties and bra, the bulge at the front of his jeans was impressive.

She nodded to it as she reached around and unhooked her bra. "I'm going to need to inspect that, too."

"I promise to let you." His thick biceps flexed and tensed, sexual tension obviously rolling through him.

Her straps slid down both arms, but she caught the bra from falling away by covering her sizable breasts with her palms. She massaged the soft lace against her sensitive nipples.

They firmed into peaks.

Ross let out a lusty, guttural sound that came from deep inside of him.

Which made her confidence soar, and she gave her breasts one more sensual squeeze, turning her nipples into stones.

She tossed the bra aside, hooked both thumbs into the thin elastic and pushed her panties down. They pooled around her ankles, and she stepped out of them.

"Fuck's sake, woman." His voice crackled with sexual electricity. "Get over here."

When she walked to him, he uncrossed his ankles so she could step between his knees. He sat up, and grasped both hips, pulling her closer. He circled her belly button with his tongue, then used the tip to toy with the gold ring.

Her eyes fluttered shut, and she wrapped her arms around his head to cradle him closer.

"That's the sexiest fucking thing I've ever seen," he whispered against her flesh. Hot, moist breaths made her skin pebble.

"You're the sexiest effing thing I've ever seen," she said into his hair.

He devoured her skin, kissing along her torso, her ribs, her hips. He found a nipple and pulled it between his teeth, worrying it until she ached with so much pleasure that she could hardly bear it. One hand stayed on her hipbone while the other smoothed down and circled her ankle. He guided her foot up to rest on the sofa. The roughness of his fingertips had her knees shaking as they trailed along the inside of her thigh and found—

"Oh, God," she gasped as his thumb circled her clit.

"No, just me." He moved his hand and sunk his teeth into the flesh around her hipbone with just enough force to make her hiss with pleasure. "But thanks for the vote of confidence."

Smartass.

She pinched his shoulder.

Just as he sank two fingers into her core and moved them in and out, rotating and circling, until her toes curled.

She whimpered and curved her nails into his shoulder.

His incredible fingers picked up speed. So did his thumb circling her nub.

"*Ross.*" Her voice was feathery and distant, almost as though it wasn't hers.

"Yes, baby." He kept nipping at her belly, kissing her flesh everywhere his mouth could reach. His tongue traced a line up between her breasts and he buried his face there, breathing her in. And those fingers. Those exquisite fingers, they kept pleasuring and pleasing until her insides quivered and quaked and she was hurtling toward the edge of heaven.

His head dipped, his mouth closed over her nub, and he sucked hard.

An orgasm so fierce and so forceful barreled through her and she unfurled, skyrocketing her into space.

"Oh, *God,* yes," he breathed against her stomach, his fingers slowed as her flesh convulsed around them.

She was still floating, unable to completely come down to Earth, when he scooped up her trembling body and laid her on the sofa.

He stepped out of his pants and boxer briefs, then retrieved a condom from his wallet.

"You're a beautiful man, you know that?" Her voice was sing-song.

"We're just getting started, babe." He had himself covered in seconds.

She opened for him as he settled between her legs. When his thick, hard shaft pulsed at her entrance, she closed her eyes.

"Look at me," he said, his voice gruff with need.

Her eyes flew open.

"I want to really *see* you when I make love to you for the first time." He circled his hips just enough to tease her. "I don't just want to see your bared body tonight. I want to see your bared soul."

That's what she was afraid of.

She drew her bottom lip between her teeth, but kept her eyes hooked into his. Without a word—because hells bells, she really couldn't speak—she gave her head the tiniest of nods.

With one swift thrust, he buried himself inside of her to the hilt.

She cried out.

He hissed in a sharp breath.

But they never broke eye contact.

He reached up and braced a hand against the arm of the sofa, then he started to ride her. Slow and gentle at first, but then faster. Harder, his pace quickening to match the building storm that reflected in his eyes.

A hurricane was swirling and building inside of her, too, and she lifted her hips to match his thrusts.

The muscle in his jaw tightened when she reached down and

grabbed his ass, pulling him deeper. He hooked an arm under the back of her knee and lifted her leg to spread her wider.

"*Yes,*" she gasped. "*Harder.*" Another gasp. "*Faster.*"

His eyes dilated, and his strokes went deeper as he rode her hard and fast. His chest brushed her breasts each time he sank into her, the friction creating an exquisite sensation.

He shifted his hips in the opposite direction, hitting just the right spot that drove her home.

She shattered into a million tiny pieces as another orgasm overtook her, pulling him into oblivion with her.

He finally let his eyes close as he pulsed inside of her. He collapsed, letting his chest press fully against hers, and the warmth of his body cocooned her.

It took a long time for their breathing to slow and their hearts to stop thundering. They laid still, soaking in the feel of skin against skin and the raw emotion that thickened the air around them. Ross turned his face into her hair and gently brushed his nose back and forth against her ear. She caressed up and down his spine with her fingertips.

It was the first time in her life she hadn't felt alone. She should be happy. Thrilled, even. Instead, she was terrified.

"Hey, big guy." She stroked his hair. The gentle cadence of his breaths told her he was content. She didn't want to ruin the moment, but she wanted him to know how sweet he'd been in the park to little Noelle, and how sorry she was that she'd run off thinking about herself instead of the pain he must've been feeling. "Know what?"

"You're perfect?" His tone was so content that she didn't want to ruin the moment by moving.

She stilled. No, no, she wasn't perfect. Not even close.

"Not what I was going to say." Her fingers moved against his hair again in soft, smooth strokes. "Guess again."

"You're not a real blonde?" He chuckled against her cheek. "I figured that out the second you dropped your panties." He nipped at her jaw.

She pinched his side.

"Ouch." He flinched.

"I was going to say something really nice, but not now." She pinched him one more time just for the hell of it. "For your information, I *am* a blonde. Just not a platinum blonde. More of a dirty blonde."

"*Oh.*" His voice went sultry with a hint of tease. "I like the dirty part."

"You're awful." She swatted his shoulder.

"Okay, it's my turn to ask a question." He lifted onto his elbows and smoothed both thumbs across her cheeks. "Tell me something."

She kept tracing his spine with her fingers.

"The little girl in the park got me to thinking..." He let a small breath slip out as he studied her. "How does a young girl survive the foster system, make it through college and law school, and become a kick ass attorney who dedicates her life to helping other people instead of thinking of herself?"

That wasn't at all what she'd been expecting him to ask, and she had to think on it for a minute.

Finally, she drew in a deep breath. "I guess foster kids develop pretty good survival instincts at a young age. There's plenty of opportunities to hone those skills. You either sink or swim, and I decided to swim. By the time I made it through undergrad, I knew I had to help kids just like me, so I went to law school. I think giving back that way came from the same survival instincts. I had to decide to either do good things with my life or bad. A lot of kids who grow up in the system make a different choice. I didn't want to end up ruining my life like my parents ruined theirs, so I focused on helping others instead of thinking of myself."

"You're incredible, you know that?" He brushed her nose with his.

She knew no such thing.

"Ross, surviving consumed me. It used all of the good parts of me."

"The things you do for kids, the pictures on your walls," he argued. "Those things say otherwise."

He didn't get it, and never would. The reason she did those things was *because* she had nothing more to offer when it came to real relationships.

He tapped a finger against her head. "I see that brilliant mind of yours working overtime."

She lifted her head to suckle his neck. "I'm thinking that I'd like a repeat performance. You're pretty good at this sex thing, you know that?"

He laughed and sat up on the edge of the sofa to grab his boxer briefs. "You deserve a real bed, so we're going to my place for round two." He stood. "I'll go find your restroom and clean up."

She watched him pad to the door, his muscled back and ass making her mouth water again. When he disappeared into the dark hallway, she whispered, "And you deserve a whole woman in your bed."

Her throat closed.

Kimberly was not intimate relationship material. Not by a long shot.

As soon as Ross figured that out, he'd leave.

And she couldn't blame him one bit for wanting someone better.

CHAPTER ELEVEN

Kimberly spent the next few days decorating the hell out of Red River. The nights at Ross's working on the wish ornaments that would decorate the tree weren't bad either.

Grinch sminch.

The glares from the residents who'd been upset with her at the council meeting had subsided as more of the decorating took shape each day.

"It's a little crooked," she cupped her gloved hands and called up to one of the firefighters Ross had called on for help.

The extra hands and their fire trucks with ladders and buckets had helped string the lights around the new tree, and hang decorations from every street lamp along Main Street. They were on the last lamp, then she could hurry back to Ross's shop to keep working on the long list of wishes that had poured into her inbox.

If she stayed up all night...

Okay, Ross was already keeping her up all night.

But if she could manage to resist that hunky body of his ... and the things he did with his fingers and tongue ... she could stay up all night working on the wishes and they'd be finished.

Once those were complete, voila. They'd be ready to light the new tree over the weekend.

She'd distributed the list of wishes to the donors, with instructions to mail the gifts to Red River by early next week or send her a pick-up address.

Ross had kept up with the carolers and Nativity characters to make sure they'd be ready, too.

Even Chairperson Clydelle had seemed impressed with their progress.

With the lighting ceremony off their overloaded plates, they could focus on getting the kids into Red River for Christmas Eve to unwrap their gifts.

Her heart warmed. Watching so many kids have their Christmas wishes come true was going to be so wonderful.

"Perfect!" Kimberly shouted when the firefighter had the decorations just right. She gave him a thumbs-up. The basket lowered. "Thanks a ton. Tomorrow around lunchtime, so we can hang the wishes on the tree?"

"Sure thing. As long as there's no fire, I'll be here." The firefighter climbed out of the basket.

As she turned to walk back down Main Street toward command central, a.k.a Ross's shop, light snow started to fall. She pulled her winter hat down over her ears and stuffed her hands in her pockets.

She stopped on the sidewalk and took in the town she'd decorated like a mad woman. Red River was a beautiful town any time of year, but she had to admit, it was so much more cheerful with all the decorations.

She'd put her whole heart into it for Ross, the same way he'd put his faith in her. She'd even been working on a huge surprise for him that she'd unveil during the tree lighting ceremony they'd scheduled.

It was going to be awesome to see the look on his face.

A door opened and out stepped one of the owners of *Shear Elegance.* "Hi, Kimberly," Dylan's fiancé, Hailey Hicks, said as she locked the door.

"Well, hey there." Kimberly smiled. "I guess I didn't realize it was getting so late." She gazed up at the overcast sky, the purple hue of dusk coloring the clouds.

"My evening clients canceled because of the storm rolling in." She tested the door of her salon to make sure it was locked. "It's not going to be a big storm, but hey, I'm not complaining. Dylan's watching our daughter at Joe's, so I can pick her up and get home early to cook dinner." Her expression fell with what seemed like guilt. "He usually has to bring dinner home since both of us work and own businesses."

Kimberly gave her a reassuring smile. "From where I stand, you're both doing a great job as parents." At least they were stepping up and trying their hardest.

Kimberly would've given the moon for at least one parent who cared enough to make an effort.

Hailey glanced down Main Street and jingled the keys in her hand. "You've got this town looking great."

"How's the wedding plans coming?" Kimberly couldn't imagine wasting money on a wedding when the justice of the peace worked just as well, but whatever. It wasn't her place to step on another gal's dream.

Hailey nodded. "They're coming, I guess. Kinda wish we would've eloped to Vegas."

Kimberly laughed.

"Hey." Hailey's forehead wrinkled. "You never took me up on the free makeover I offered you several months ago."

Kimberly hadn't had a reason to get a makeover. Until now.

She stared at the sidewalk for a second. "Could I take you up on that day after tomorrow? We're lighting the Wishing Tree that night, and I'd like to look nice." For a change.

They set a time, and Kimberly strolled along Main Street, crossed over at an intersection, and started whistling ... *Frosty the Snowman?*

Oh jeez. She was becoming a Christmas sap just like Ross.

Guess that's what great sex and love did to a gal.

She stopped in her tracks. Couldn't make a sound, as though

she'd been chewing dry crackers with no water to wash them down.

A hand went to her throat and she massaged so she could actually swallow.

She loved Ross.

Holy shit, s*he loved Ross.*

Fear lanced through her, and she felt like a scared little girl all over again. She pushed those fears aside, and slowly forced one foot in front of the other until his shop came into view. Darkness hadn't completely fallen over Red River, but his Christmas lights blinked on, and she couldn't stop a smile.

She entered the building, taking off her coat and winter gear as she followed the hallway that emptied into the back area where he worked on cars. And found herself alone.

A voice came from the back corner office. She laid her jacket on a bench and eased in the direction of the office. She peeked around the corner, and Ross was on the phone, sitting at his desk, with his back to the door.

"What the hell, Frank? You promised me those buses. You can't pull out *now.*" Ross went quiet, listening with the landline phone to his ear. "Listen." His voice was angry. "I've given my word to the most important person in my life, and I am not going to let her down just because some rich asshat flashed a lot of money under your nose to get you to bus his entire neighborhood to a pro football game. Tell him to find another way to show off how fucking rich he is."

Kimberly's chest tightened.

Ross went quiet, listening again. "Watch your mouth, Frank. She's not just a *squeeze.* You have no idea what this woman does for other people." Ross ran his fingers through his hair. "Or how much she means to me. She's more special than you and me put together, and I don't want to disappoint her."

Kimberly blinked. Then blinked again.

The tightness in her chest released, only for butterfly wings to beat against her ribcage.

"Oh yeah? Well, don't come crying to me the next time your fifteen million-dollar classic Aston Martin needs work, or I swear to God I'll tear out the engine block and return it to you with nothing under the hood." He slammed down the phone and raked a hand over his face.

She gave him a few minutes, then she rapped a knuckle against the open door. "Hey, big guy."

He spun around in his executive's chair. "Hey, you." A forced smile turned up his lips, but there was no happiness in his eyes. "How'd it go with the street lamp decorations?"

"It went awesome, thanks to you enlisting the fire department." She walked to him. "Several firefighters even offered to drive the moving truck when they're off duty to pick up the donated gifts that aren't going to be mailed here."

"Good." He hooked fingers into her belt loops and pulled her close. "I'm glad to hear they came through, because I work on their cars for free."

"So, I'm not the only community do-gooder around?" She slid one knee onto the chair, then the other, straddling him.

He smirked. "For all the good it's doing me. I've got bad news."

She placed a finger to his lips. "Shhhh. I don't want bad news. My life has mostly been bad news. You can tell me tomorrow. Right now, I just want to focus on good things." She circled her hips and felt him grow hard against her center.

"And here I thought you showed up to work on more wishes for the tree." He placed a hand at the back of her head and pulled her mouth within a breath of his.

"I did," she whispered. "But I also showed up to screw your brains out first."

A wicked smile curved onto his lips, and that time it *did* reflect in his eyes. "That sounds so damn sexy that I think I just forgot my fucking name."

He stood, lifting her with him, and turned to the side. With one arm, he started to swipe at the top of the desk, then he stopped. "Can't damage these." He picked up a framed photo of a young tween-age girl wearing a Santa hat and sat it on the filing cabinet next to his desk.

"Noelle?" Kimberly asked. As much time as she'd been spending at his shop, they'd been too busy working on the decorations for her to peruse the photos on his desk.

He nodded.

"She was so cute," Kimberly whispered, playing with the ends of his hair at the back of his neck.

"My sister was definitely cute." He grabbed another frame, turning it so Kimberly could see the photo. It was a picture of her in his truck the day they'd driven out to the wilderness to search for the first Wishing Tree.

"You had it framed," she said, a little in awe at how sentimental he was. She'd stopped getting attached to photos or any other personal belongings before she'd reached puberty.

"How could I not? The girl in this photo is hot as sin." Comet was behind her in the front seat, trying to make out with her cheek and ear. Kimberly's face was crinkled up in an expression that said *ewww, gross*.

Kimberly belly laughed. "That dog should be registered as a sex offender. That's one wicked tongue he's got on him."

"I've got a pretty wicked tongue, myself. All the better to lick you with, my dear." Ross's eyebrows bounced up and down. "Can you wear a red cape with a hood for me one night?"

She cocked her head to one side. "Ah, so the truth comes out about Red River's most famous mechanic, who seems perfect and above reproach in public. In private, you have a Little Red Riding Hood fantasy."

His eyes turned smoky. "It's only my fantasy if *you're* in it and you don't have anything else on besides the cape." He squinted up at the ceiling thoughtfully. "Unless you can put on red high heels, too. Red stilettos would definitely have a place in my fantasies."

She swatted his shoulder.

He set her picture with Comet on the filing cabinet along with his sister's. Then he picked up one last frame.

"I just had your photo and this sketch framed yesterday." It was the drawing she'd scratched out on paper of Comet the same day he'd taken her photo with the pervy but lovable mutt.

The gesture to frame both was so wonderfully sweet that it turned her insides to mush.

She laid a kiss on him that turned the insides of her eyelids white.

He set the frame with the others. With the back of one forearm, he made a pass across the desk and sent papers, message pads, and pens flying. "We'll start here."

They started and finished. Twice.

Then they went to his cabin and worked on glittery snowflake ornaments, which each had a child's name and their wish written on it in bold red and green marker.

In the wee hours of the morning, after they were done with the snowflakes, they went to bed, and *finished* at least two more times.

———

"You had *one* job." Kimberly all but stomped into Angelique's office early Saturday morning to blow off steam. To blow off the fear of falling in love with Ross and leaving herself open to potential heartache. Worse, leaving him open to finally figuring out how broken she really was.

Later that night, they were officially lighting the Wishing Tree. The entire town was decorated like the North Pole. The snowflake ornament wishes adorned the tree, courtesy of the Red River Fire Department.

Miraculously, Chairperson Clydelle and her sidekick sister had given their stamp of approval on all the decorations.

Deacon West hadn't even put up a fuss when they'd broken the news to him that the buses had fallen through, and they'd have to go back to their original plan to bring the gifts to the kids. How could he complain, after the shenanigans in the park that resulted in a ruined tree and a vandalized Nativity scene. She still had the moving truck she'd borrowed, and the fire fighters had offered to make the rounds to make sure every wish was delivered.

All in all, it had been a kick ass couple of days.

Yet Kimberly had still managed an epic fail.

She'd fallen for Ross, and Ross had fallen for her.

She flung herself into the armchair in front of the desk.

Angelique didn't look up from her computer. "*Aaaand* here we go again," she mumbled.

"One job." Kimberly held up an index finger and let her eyes bug out. "Was that too much to ask?"

Angelique stopped typing, slowly took off her glasses, and swiveled to look at Kimberly. "Apparently, it was." She fiddled with her glasses. "Especially since I'm not aware of a job I was supposed to be doing." She waved a hand over the stacks of papers on her desk. "Other than working my ass off to keep this office afloat while you decorate a town for a holiday that you don't even like all that much."

"I had no choice!" Kimberly let her arms fall over the sides of the chair. "You said so yourself, right after I bombed at the town council meeting. Ms. Clydelle would've stalked me with her gavel and cane if I hadn't agreed, and you know it." She let out a huge Oscar-worthy sigh. "*You're* the one who told me I should go ahead and do this instead of standing up to that old hen."

Angelique pursed her lips. "True on all accounts." She tapped her reading glasses against the desk. "Refresh my memory. What job have I failed to perform?"

Kimberly covered her face with both hands. She couldn't look her bestie in the eye when she fessed up to her lapse in self-control. "You were supposed to keep me from falling in love."

The silence was deafening.

She spread her fingers and peeked at Angelique, who looked dumbstruck.

"Well?" Kimberly huffed. "Say something."

It took Angelique a moment to respond. "First..." Her voice

was scary quiet. "You never asked me to stop you from falling in love."

"I thought it was a given!" Kimberly dragged her hands down her face. "You're the one who chose to hyphenate your name so it's as long as a Latin disease. After you did that, I *told* you my name wouldn't fit on the door if I ever got married."

Angelique's forehead wrinkled. "Um ... I'm so lost right now. Who are you in love with and when are you two getting married?" She frowned. "And what in God's name does our office door have to do with this?"

Kimberly picked at a cuticle. "Okay, I'm *not* getting married, so I guess the door is a non-issue." *Pick, pick, pick.*

"And?" Angelique lifted a brow.

"I guess I'm sort of in love with Ross." Kimberly kept her head lowered, but stopped the cuticle picking long enough to lift her gaze to look at her friend through shuttered lashes.

A wicked *pay-backs-are-a-bitch* smile spread across Angelique's face.

A few years ago, Kimberly distinctly remembered telling her bestie she was being ridiculous for not wanting to fall in love with Dr. Tall, Dark, and Hotsome.

"Thanks a lot," Kimberly groused.

Angelique's chair creaked as she leaned back and swiveled from one side to the other. "So, the sexy mechanic is the one who finally brought the invincible Kimberly Perez to her knees."

In more ways than one.

Heat crept up Kimberly's neck and settled in her cheeks because she actually had been on her knees in front of Ross. A few times. One of which had been last night in the shower.

Her cheeks burned hot.

She studied a photo of the Italian countryside that was hanging on Angelique's wall. Rolling hills covered in grapevines were on fire with the colors of autumn.

"Oh. My. God," Angelique said on a low laugh. "You've been dirty dancing with Ross!"

Kimberly's BFF knew her too damn well. "Fine." She threw her head back to rest against the chair. "Yes, we're doing the dance." On her office sofa. On his desk. In his bed.

Okay, fine. Even once in his truck when they were scouting for a new tree in the wilderness. She'd frozen her bare cheeks off, too, thank you very much.

But it had been *sooooooo* worth it.

With each passing day, the butterflies that fluttered in her chest every time she saw him ... or even thought of him, had turned to full grown birds with wings that didn't just flutter. They flapped and beat against her chest until she couldn't breathe.

"So, what am I going to do about the mess I'm in?" she asked, completely defeated. "I've even been working on a surprise for him of legendary proportions, which is going to blow his mind." Not something she'd ever done for a man. But for Ross?

Least she could do after all the mind-blowing sex he'd given her. It had taken her two years to finally take that step with him, and lucky girl that she was, the guy was really, really good at it. She couldn't get enough of him.

She groaned as though she was in agony.

Angelique's smirk turned to sympathy. "Hon, you're over-thinking this because you're scared."

Funny, Ross had said the same thing.

"You seem happy." Angelique's smile was back. "Not quite as terrifying."

"Some friend you are." Kimberly ran her fingers through her hair, then she pointed to it. "*This* hasn't even scared him away yet."

"That's because he's a solid guy." Angelique looked thoughtful. "Here's an idea." She tapped her chin. "How about just roll with it? Enjoy the moment. Stop worrying and let life happen."

Kimberly rubbed her eyes. "Life has happened way too much for me already. That's why I took charge at twelve years old and decided I'd control who I let myself care about."

Angelique swiveled back and forth again. "And how has that worked out for you so far?"

"Well…" It hadn't worked out at all, actually. Unless being alone and lonely … and kind of pathetic was her goal.

She hadn't been aiming for pathetic. Unfortunately, she'd accomplished alone, lonely, *and* pathetic like a champ.

Until Ross had come along and had the audacity to be a standup guy.

Kimberly focused on her sparkly Christmas green nail polish that she'd picked up at the pharmacy the night before. The bottle had actually had the picture of a Grinch on it, so, of course, she'd had to buy it.

Ross had belly laughed when she'd brushed it on her fingers and toes. Then, as soon as it was dry, he'd started at her green fingernails and kissed all the way to her green toenails, lingering for a long time at several points in between.

Amazing that they'd actually been able to finish the wish ornaments.

She drew in a dramatic breath, then let it out, puffing out her cheeks.

Maybe instead of worrying about disappointing him, or waiting for him to disappoint her, she should focus on trying to be the kind of woman he deserved.

Her breath caught in her throat.

No, that wasn't exactly true.

Maybe she should finally focus on being the kind of person *she* deserved. That kind of person would let themselves be loved, wouldn't they?

She shot out of the chair, ran around the desk, and gave Angelique a big kiss on the top of her head. "Thanks. I knew I could count on you for help."

"Um, okay." Angelique's look said she was more confused than ever.

"No time to explain." Kimberly waved her hand in the air. "I have an appointment at *Shear Elegance* before we light the tree tonight."

Angelique's brows lifted so high they disappeared under her jet-black hair. "No more do-it-yourself dye jobs? No more cutting your own hair?" She let out a low whistle. "You *must* be in love, girlfriend."

"Oh, bite me," Kimberly groused.

"You don't need me for that," Angelique shot back. "The hickey on your neck says Ross already has it covered."

Kimberly's hand flew to her neck. "I have a hickey?"

Angelique let out a laugh that filled the room. Then she went back to typing. "See you tonight in the park."

Kimberly hurried out of the office. If she didn't slow her pace, she could swing by her place before her makeover appointment and change out of her Christmas sweatshirt into a turtle neck to cover the mark on her neck.

She kept a hand over her neck as she flew down the stairs. She hadn't bothered to look in the mirror when she showered and got dressed that morning. Ross was going to catch hell for not telling her he'd given her a hickey for all the world to see.

Then she was going to kiss the hell out of him and give him a hickey or two of his own.

CHAPTER TWELVE

By the time the sun disappeared behind Wheeler Peak, the park was full of people who'd come to see the lighting of the Wishing Tree.

Ross glanced around, taking it all in as he let out a sigh of relief. The town decked out in Christmas splendor with fresh snow on the ground and the townsfolk turning out to participate—that was the heart of Red River. It was the heart of the holidays.

His sister would've been thrilled.

He gazed up, and a shooting star streaked across the night sky. His heart warmed. It was as though Noelle was telling him she was pleased with him.

He closed his eyes and wished on that star, the way he and Noelle used to do when they were kids. His wish was for his parents to someday enjoy Christmas and remember Noelle during the holidays instead of trying harder to forget her because of their consuming grief.

He opened his eyes again to check on all the moving parts that would make tonight a success.

Both the live Nativity scene and the carolers were in full costume. Deacon West had even made sure to include real hay and two live miniature donkeys. Even the baby in the manger was a doll that looked as lifelike as possible. The bonus, though, was the kids who'd likely vandalized Ross's scrap iron sculptures. Apparently, Deacon West must've suspected they'd been the culprits, too, because he was in the process of handing each of them pooper scoopers to clean up after the animals.

Ross chuckled.

He found Dylan McCoy at the front southeast corner of the park handing out free hot chocolate, courtesy of Cotton Eyed Joe's.

"Thanks, man." Ross hitched up his chin at Dylan's table. "This is a really nice touch."

Dylan handed him a cup, steam swirling up into the cold night air. "Sure thing. Least I can do after you and Kimberly pulled this off so spectacularly."

A family of four came up the sidewalk and approached Dylan's table. He handed each of them full cups.

"Enjoy the evening, folks," Ross said.

They thanked both him and Dylan and strolled into the park.

"Gotta say." Dylan filled more cups and set them out on the table. "I'm surprised and impressed."

Ross had to agree. Then again, Kimberly never ceased to surprise or impress him.

He took in the bustling park while he sipped his warm cocoa. Little Noelle's foster mom led her to the tree, where she put something on it. Ross couldn't make out exactly what it was, but the color was bright yellow. Then Noelle's foster mom led her away.

Sorrow filled his chest, but then he swallowed it down with another big gulp of cocoa. He wouldn't let grief ruin this night, the way his parents let grief ruin every night and every holiday since his sister had passed.

He finished his drink, tossed it in the trash, and shook Dylan's hand. "Thanks, man. Gotta go get busy." He nodded toward the unlit tree, then went to inspect it.

It was fully decorated with the recycled lights he and Kimberly had collected and the snowflake wishes they'd made every night in between all of their other planning, their other responsibilities, and ... well, all of their extraordinary lovemaking.

The sheer number of snowflakes alone was a testament to Kimberly's commitment to underprivileged kids because they each represented a Christmas gift that a child in need had wished for.

There were so many, and Kimberly had made sure every last wish would come true. The same way she'd made his wish come true, and not just with the wonderfully decorated town.

She'd made his wish to have her in his life come true. She'd given him a chance, and finally let him through the crazy hair, the wild clothes, and the tough-girl shell so he could see into her heart. A heart that was far bigger than her larger-than-life personality.

Beautifully wrapped gifts to fulfill the wishes were pouring into the Red River Post Office every day by the truckloads. Local firefighters had picked up several loads from donors, and Ross's shop was overflowing with presents.

He hadn't been able to solve the problem of getting the kids to Red River, thanks to his client reneging on his promise to loan him a fleet of luxury buses. But the Red River Fire Department had stepped up again. Their off-duty firefighters had offered to drive the moving truck around the state and hand deliver the gifts.

So tonight, he and Kimberly could enjoy watching the tree light up, knowing that her wish to see so many kids receive a Christmas gift would come true.

In the midst of all the sparkly snowflake ornaments was a bright yellow star with child-like writing on it. It had been placed on the bottom branches, right about eye level with a little girl named Noelle. Ross reached for the yellow star to see if he could make out the writing on it, but before he picked it up, Calvin Wells' head appeared from around the side of the tree.

"Hey, dude." Cal, the newest member of the Red River Fire Department, said. "Got a sec?"

Ross followed him to the rear of the tree, where Cal and another firefighter were manning the electrical outlet that would light up the tree. "We're almost ready. Have you seen Kimberly?" Cal's hair was trimmed to perfection. He was somewhere between early to mid-twenties, but looked younger. Almost like a boy scout because of his combed hair and cleanly shaven face. Cal's older brother, Cooper Wells, was Red River's only chiropractor, and his sister-in-law was the infamous erotic romance author who'd kept her identity a secret ... until she didn't, which has rocked the cozy little town.

Ross chuckled at the memory. For a small town, Red River had a lot of interesting history behind it. Stories of scandals, secret love affairs, dangerous arsonists, and so much more. Honestly, someone should write a book about all of it. Because, really, who could make that shit up?

Ross shook his head. "I was going to ask you the same question. You haven't seen her?"

Cal shook his head and kept checking the power connections. "No, dude. She hasn't been around all afternoon."

Huh.

The decorations, the tree ... they were mostly her doing. For someone who'd wanted to eliminate decorations altogether, she'd done an amazing job turning Red River into a town that Santa himself would envy, and she'd done it at virtually no cost.

Amazing.

She was amazing.

She was also missing-in-action.

"We wanted her stamp of approval on the last decoration she had us add to the tree." Cal walked around to the side of the tree and pointed to a large arch that was secured in the middle. It was covered in burlap, with pull-strings on each side.

He didn't remember Kimberly working on a decoration shaped like an arch. "What is it?"

Call glanced up from his work. "Can't tell you. That's why I'm looking for Kimberly."

Ross frowned. "Why the hell can't you tell me? I'm in charge of this gig."

Not really. Kimberly was more the boss than he was, but he wanted to know what was so important that it had to be covered.

Cal shook his head and went back to working on the electrical cords. "No can do, dude. You're only one of the people in charge of this gig. The other one has wild hair and threatened to find me in my sleep, tie me up, and wax the hair off my balls if I gave up her secret."

Ouch.

Cal and his firefighting helper both shuddered.

Ross couldn't blame them. The threat did sound like something Kimberly would say, even though he knew she'd never do any such thing.

What kind of secret had Kimberly been keeping, though? And why? Ross studied the covered arch hanging on the tree.

He couldn't stop a wide smile. Threatening a young guy with hot wax was exactly the kind of thing that had made Ross fall in love with her.

He swallowed.

Yeah. Man up, dude. He was in love with a woman who was going to keep him so far up on his toes that he might as well get used to wearing steel-toed boots. Even to bed and in the shower.

Especially to bed and in the shower.

He took out his phone and checked the time because it was getting late. He fired off a text.

Where are you?

The dots jumped.

Be there soon, big guy.

He typed a response.

When???? Everything's ready.

The dots did their dance.

Not everything. It's not quite dark, and I'm not there, am I?

He responded right away.

Exactly. You're holding up the tree lighting, so get your pretty little ass over here ASAP.

The dots jumped.

You think my ass is pretty?

He fired off another text.

Damn sure do. Now get it to the park. It'll be dark in a few minutes.

She responded just as fast.

Bully. On my way.

She was an exasperating woman.

He drew cold air into his lungs for patience because a serious relationship with her was going to require a lot of grit. Grit was something he had a lot of, thank God. Besides, now that they finally were in a serious relationship, he planned to love every minute of it.

Well, maybe not every minute. Especially if he ever made her angry enough to threaten him with hot wax. If that ever happened, he was confident enough in his skills in the sack to soften her foul mood.

He turned to go check with Deacon West on the Nativity scene.

And bumped right into his parents.

"Mom. Dad." Ross was stunned.

His mother's usual sad look only deepened when she took in all the festivities and cheerful decorations. Both of them had aged tremendously after Noelle's death, but they looked even older since the last time Ross had seen them. His father's hair was nearly white. The lines around his mom's mouth and eyes had tripled in number and size.

"What are you doing here?" Ross asked.

"We were invited." His dad placed an arm around his mom.

It took a moment for his dad's comment to register. "Who invited you?" Ross was going to hunt the sorry shit down and make sure they knew how much pain they'd caused his parents. And how much pain their presence would cause Ross, too. Their grief made him feel like he was drowning every time he was around them, which was why he didn't go around them much. Whoever extended the invitation to his folks on that particular night was going to catch hell, because their attendance was going to ruin the experience for Ross. Their constant grief had ruined every holiday for Ross since Noelle had been gone.

His dad pointed over Ross's shoulder. "Your friend invited us."

Ross whirled to deliver a scalding rant to the fool who'd over-stepped their bounds so badly that they were about to get their ass handed to them.

Instead, his jaw dropped to the ground.

"Kimberly?" His voice was a thready whisper.

She strolled right up to him. "Yep. It's me, big guy."

Her hair wasn't platinum anymore. It also wasn't short. It was closer to his sandy blond color, and hung past her shoulders in long, loose curls. She had on makeup ... and deep Christmas red lipstick that made him want to rub it off with his own lips.

He couldn't unhook his gaze from those sensual red lips, and she touched them with her fingers, her nails painted a sparkly Christmas green.

Sexier still were the long eyelashes—new since he'd seen her earlier that day when they'd had incredible morning sex, then she'd showered and dressed in a hurry without even looking in the mirror to find the hickey he'd playfully given her in bed. The long silky lashes brushed her soft creamy skin as she let her eyes open and close.

"You look..."

Amazing. Incredible. Beautiful.

She pulled a bright red bottom lip between her teeth, her expression turning to uncertainty as she waited for him to finish.

"Different," Ross blurted.

Her expression blanked.

Fuck's sake. He was still rattled by his parents' surprise appearance.

He took Kimberly's arm and tugged her a few steps away. "I mean you look fabulous, but what happened to your hair?" Was that him talking? Because that probably wasn't the response a woman would be looking for. His mind was still spinning because of his parents showing up at a holiday event unexpectedly.

Kimberly ran a hand over the long locks, her hand tremoring. "I ... I had a makeover and went back to my natural color." Her voice shook a little. "My stylist added extensions to my hair." She batted her eyes. "And to my eyelashes." She leaned in and whispered, "You don't like it?"

Her tone, and her expression, said she was insecure about her new appearance, and he wanted to kick his own ass for making it worse with his brash comments.

"I love it." He kept his voice low. "It's just that ... I..." Shit, he couldn't get his brain to connect with his fucking mouth because he was so thrown. "I'm just surprised. You look ... great ... you always look great, so why did you—"

A throat cleared, and Ross turned back to his parents.

Shit, his *parents*. They were there. At a Christmas tree lighting ceremony.

Jesus.

He glanced around the park, his teeth grinding to dust. Where was the inconsiderate bonehead who'd asked his mom and dad to come to the tree lighting?

Kimberly stepped around him to stand at his side.

"I'm sorry, Mom and Dad." Ross pinched the bridge of his nose. "This is Kimberly." He pulled her flush against his side, craning his neck around to find the so-called friend his parents had pointed to.

No one was close. They must've been pointing across the park.

"Nice to meet you, since our son hasn't brought you over to introduce you himself." His mom gave him a thin smile, then turned a crusty look on Kimberly. "Thank you for calling us. I'm sure you meant well, but this really isn't the best ... environment for us..." Her voice cracked. Her eyes teared up, and she covered her mouth with a cupped hand.

Wait.

His gaze fell to Kimberly. "*You* invited them?"

She nodded and gave him another shy bat of her new eyelashes. "Surprise, big guy." She motioned to the firefighters.

The tree lights sprung to life, and the entire park went quiet in awe.

Kimberly motioned again, the firefighters walked to the covered decoration on the tree, and they pulled the cords.

The burlap fell away.

Ross's heart dropped to his feet.

His mom gasped and covered her mouth with a shaky hand.

The arch that had been covered was a wooden sign with holly leaves and red letters painted onto it.

The sign read *Noelle's Wishing Tree*.

His mom choked back a sob.

"Mom," Ross rasped out. "I'm so sorry."

"What's wrong?" Creases formed across Kimberly's forehead. "I ... I wanted to surprise you by dedicating the tree to your sister." She waved a hand at the sign, then leaned in to whisper to Ross, "I thought it would be a nice gesture for you and your parents. You don't like this either?"

"No, I sure as hell don't," he ground out. "My parents don't celebrate the holidays, Kimberly."

Her usual gigantic personality and outgoing countenance were gone, just as much as her wild hair and crazy clothes. He literally didn't recognize the person in front of him who'd been thoughtless enough to do something so callous.

"I..." Her eyes rounded to the size of the moon. She leaned in to whisper so only he could hear. "You said they hadn't done their part to carry out your sister's last wishes. You never me told they didn't celebrate Christmas at all, Ross. I thought it would be special for you." Her brows pulled together.

"Special for me or you?" He stepped away from her. "You're the one who wanted this tree, not me." He glanced at his parents and their grief hit him like a tidal wave. Pulled him under all over again. "Why would you do this?" he hissed out, leaning in so only she could hear. "I told you how my parents are when it comes to my sister."

"Ross, I had no idea. I thought this would *help*." Kimberly's chin quivered. "I'm sor—"

"Hi, mister," a tiny voice said as someone tugged on his pants leg.

Ross looked down. *And the hits just keep on coming.*

Little Noelle was standing in front of him, between him and his parents. "Thank you for all the lights so Santa can find us." She looked up at him with a bright, dazzling smile. She pointed to the bright yellow star she'd put on the tree. "I wished for a mommy and daddy."

"*Noelle.*" Her foster mom ran over and took her hand.

Ross's mom burst into tears.

Noelle's foster mom looked from Ross's angry face, to Kimberly's stunned expression. Then to his parents' grief that had his mom crumpled against his father's side.

"I'm so sorry to interrupt." Noelle's foster mom led her away.

"We should go," said his dad. He led Ross's mom toward the street.

"Mom. Dad!" Ross called after them, but his dad just waved him off over one shoulder and kept walking toward the street.

"How could you be so thoughtless?" Ross turned on Kimberly.

Her lips parted on a rush of air. "I'm sorry. You said they still struggled with your sister's loss. I didn't know they'd react like this—"

"Of course you didn't, because you didn't bother to ask." Ross ran his fingers through his hair. "You just go through life saying whatever you want, letting anything and everything pop out of that no-filtered mouth of yours. Do you have any idea how much pain you just caused them? How much you just caused *me*?"

"I ... I didn't mean to—"

"Well, you did." He raked a hand over his face. "Now I've got to go clean up this mess and hope my parents will speak to me again in this century." He took a step in the direction his parents had left, but then he stopped. "You'll have to handle the rest of this fiasco on your own. I've got my own problems to deal with now, and I've had enough of..." He studied her for a moment, then waved a hand at the Wishing Tree. "I've had enough of *this*."

He turned and ate up the ground with long strides to go find his broken-hearted parents, and hope that Kimberly's colossal mistake didn't set them back another decade and prevent them from recovering from their grief.

CHAPTER THIRTEEN

Kimberly watched Ross disappear into the darkness.

The wetness in her eyes blurred her vision as she glanced around the park.

Even with most of Red River's residents milling around, enjoying the tree, the Nativity scene, the carolers, and free hot chocolate, she found herself totally alone.

Some things never changed.

Watching people turn their backs on her and walk away because she was either too much or not enough was something she'd seen a thousand times.

Never again.

This would be the *last* time.

She gave herself a moment. Then she drew in a deep breath and got her shit together. Mostly.

She gathered enough nerve to at least finish her task of making the kids' wishes come true, which had been her original intent anyway. So really, she was just back to square one.

Getting kicked to the curb by another unreliable adult didn't matter.

That was her story, anyway, and she was sticking to it.

She darted through the crowd, looking for the postmaster.

Finally, she found her knocking back hot chocolate with Chairperson Clydelle and Ms. Francine, just as a silver flask disappeared into Ms. Francine's dangling purse.

"Good evening, ladies." Kimberly focused on the postmaster. "Thank you for the extra work you've had to do with all the packages. Can you deliver the rest to my office instead of *Ross's Automotive?*"

"Sure, if that's what you'd like." The postmaster nodded, her curly hair brushing her shoulders. Then she hiccupped and pressed her fingertips to her lips.

"You've done a fantastic job, dear," Ms. Francine said to Kimberly, drawing her attention away from the sauced postmaster. "I still think the big balls would've been more festive, but this is nice, too."

Kimberly tried to smile.

"Why do you want the packages going to your office?" Ms. Clydelle asked, leaning on her cane. "Seems there's more room at Ross's shop."

Because she wasn't welcome there anymore. Because he'd left her, and anyone who would leave her once would do it again, so he wouldn't get another chance.

"It's ... just easier for me, that's all. I've decided to deliver the packages myself." Kimberly stuffed her hands in her pockets. "Ross has other priorities now that Red River is decorated to his liking."

"Well," Ms. Clydelle said. "All you and Mr. Armstrong have left to accomplish is delivering the gifts to the kids..." She tapped her cane against the ground. "Or is it the kids are coming here? Refresh my memory."

"Ross tried to bring the kids to Red River, but due to circumstances beyond his control, that's not going to happen. It's not his fault." Why was Kimberly defending him? It was the truth, though, and she couldn't lie. "I'll make sure the gifts arrive at their proper destinations." She would not let those kids down, if it was the last good thing she did in her life.

"Lovely hair, by the way," said Ms. Clydelle. "Did it work?"

"Um, excuse me?" Kimberly asked.

"Did your fella like the change?" Ms. Francine blinked behind thick glasses.

It would seem not. "Honestly, I don't care. I only know that I don't like it because it's not me."

"Are you all right, dear?" Ms. Clydelle adjusted her cane.

Just grand. "Yep. Perfect." Kimberly thumped her chest. "No worries here." She would not feel sorry for herself. She took a step back. "Well, gotta fly like Santa." She waggled fingers toward the sky. "Gifts to deliver and all that."

"One more thing, dear." Ms. Clydelle held up her cup of spiked cocoa. "I saw the Armstrongs were here when you dedicated the tree to their daughter. You did the right thing."

Kimberly's throat grew thick. "Apparently not, because I caused a wonderful family even more pain."

Ms. Clydelle thumped her cane. "No, hon. You didn't cause them pain. They've been wallowing in it for a long time. I can't imagine what they've gone through. I never lost a child, but I've lost a husband way too young." She waved her cane at her sister. "So did Francine."

Francine nodded. "I was never able to have kids at all. They had a daughter whose loss was so unfair. But they *did* have her, and by trying to forget her memory altogether, they're missing the whole point of her life. They needed someone to remind them of that, and Ross has been shouldering the burden of trying to move on for as long as I can remember."

Kimberly's heart skipped a beat, compassion welling up inside of her.

She shook her head. He'd still walked away the first time she made a major mistake, when she'd been trying to help heal their wounds. He'd left the second they hit a rough patch. If there was one thing she'd learned growing up in the system, it was that when the times got tough, the not-so-tough got going and left her to fend for herself.

When she kept shaking her head, unable to find words, both sisters sighed.

"Well, we tried." Ms. Clydelle said it more to her sister than to Kimberly.

"Yes, we did." Ms. Francine rested her cup against the top of her purse. "To think I could've gone ahead and ordered those big balls. Getting these two hardheaded youngsters to admit they belong together was all for nothing."

Wait. *What?*

"We didn't need new decorations," Ms. Clydelle started fussing at her sister. "The other decorations are fine. I bet we get at least five more years out of them."

"Are you..." She looked around and lowered her voice. "Are you *shitting* me?" she hissed. "You two set this up to play matchmaker?" She didn't wait for them to answer. "Do you have any idea how much trouble you've caused both me and Ross?"

Not so much as a twinkle of guilt appeared in their eyes.

"That's our job in this town, dear," Ms. Francine said. "We've never been wrong about a couple until now."

Kimberly threw up her hands and marched out of the park. She went straight to Ross's shop and backed the moving truck into the garage. She hurried to load the gifts so she'd be gone by the time he returned from chasing down his parents.

His hurting, grieving parents.

Which she'd caused. Unknowingly, of course.

She'd thought she was helping. Thought she was doing something special for Ross, the way he'd helped make her dream come true to provide Christmas gifts to so many kids in unfortunate circumstances.

Wow. That had worked out *so* well, maybe she should visit a children's hospital next and remind the parents that their kids were dangerously ill while passing out teddy bears with broken hearts stitched onto the front.

Because that was about all she'd accomplished by inviting

Ross's parents to the park, then dedicating the Wishing Tree to their daughter.

The fact that a little foster girl named Noelle had walked up at the worst possible moment had to be the most unfortunate coincidence in the history of absurdly disastrous coincidences.

And all because two meddling meddling sisters—who also had good intentions, so bless their little old hearts—took it upon themselves to pimp out the single adults of Red River.

Kimberly loaded faster, darting from the pile of gifts to the truck and back again.

She probably shouldn't blame Ross for leaving her.

But yes. Yes, she did. He could've stuck around a little longer. Given her a chance to explain. Maybe even forgiven her because she hadn't meant to hurt anyone, especially him and his parents. How was she supposed to know his parents didn't celebrate Christmas? He'd left that tidbit of 4-1-1 out when he'd poured out his heart about his parents' grief.

She kept loading the gifts at lightning speed.

Just as most everyone else in her life had done since the day she landed in foster care, Ross had given up on her the moment she made a mistake.

By the time she had the last of the gifts loaded, she was sweating from lifting and toting the gifts, from hopping into the truck with them, then running back to grab more.

When she was finally done, she didn't waste any time. She secured the doors of the truck, opened the garage bay, and pulled out of their makeshift headquarters without stopping to close the garage door.

Turning onto Main Street, she drove away from *Ross's Automotive*.

Drove away from Ross.

Without a backward glance, she drove up Main Street, turned left onto a side street just past her office, then pulled into the parking lot behind their office complex. She took the stairs two at a time, throwing the door open as soon as she could get it unlocked, and beelined it straight to her office for a pair of scissors.

She clipped and snipped until all the hair extensions were laying in the sink.

When she was done, she looked down at her matchy-matchy clothes. So, they were mostly black, because that was the easiest color to coordinate with, but still. She would get rid of those when she got back to her place.

Okay, maybe she'd keep the clothes. They *did* make her feel good.

But the hair extensions? She was going to have a bonfire with those suckers.

She grabbed a rag from the cabinet and scrubbed off every remnant of stupid makeup and ridiculous red lipstick. Unfortunately, she'd have to have the lashes removed at *Shear Elegance* after she was done with her road trip to deliver the gifts, but she dug through her purse and found the Grinch green nail polish. With a dunk shot, it hit the trash can dead center.

Score.

Rummaging through every cabinet and drawer, she finally slammed the last one shut.

Dammit, why hadn't she kept an extra do-it-yourself dye kit at the office for nights like tonight?

She froze and stared at her cropped hair and plain face in the mirror. And finally let the pieces of her broken heart start to fall apart one tiny sliver at a time.

Tears slipped down her cheeks, but she swiped them away, and buried the rest of the tears the same way she'd had to do when leaving every foster home and every school to move on to the next.

To hell with keeping extra dye kits handy at the office.

"There will *never* be another night like tonight." In a low, controlled voice, that didn't sound at all like herself, she made herself that promise. Promises were usually broken in her experience. But unlike just about every person she'd come across in her life who broke the promises they'd made to her, she'd keep that one.

She'd make damn sure of it.

———

Ross sat outside of his parents' house in his old classic pickup for a long, long time.

He needed to think. Think about his parents and the pain they must've felt when they saw the Wishing Tree sign with Noelle's name on it. Think about how that pain must've crushed them all over again when a little girl named Noelle walked up and said she'd wished for parents. Think about Kimberly and what she'd done.

Think about how much he must've hurt her because of the things he'd said.

He leaned forward and tapped his head against the steering wheel.

He'd waited two years for Kimberly to open up to him, and then in record time, he'd destroyed his chance to show her she could count on him.

Talk about a Grinch.

He was Grinch, Scrooge, and the Abominable Snow Monster all in one.

By the time he was finally ready to confront his folks, frost had started to accumulate on the windshield.

He trekked across the snow-covered walkway up to the front door and knocked.

A few moments went by with no sound coming from inside. Just when he was about to give up, the door cracked.

"Ross," his dad said, then unhooked the chain latch and opened the door wide. "Come in. You don't have to knock, son."

"Yeah, Dad." Ross brushed past his father. "Unfortunately, I do. That's what I came to talk about with you and Mom."

His dad walked toward the den, waving Ross to follow.

His mother was in a recliner that rocked, covered in a

crocheted afghan, staring into the fire. She looked up and a barely-there smile appeared on her lips that didn't reflect the desolation in her eyes. "Hi, son." She motioned to the sofa. "Take off your coat and have a seat."

"I'll sit, but I'm not staying long." He kept his coat on and claimed a spot on the sofa. The brown paneling made the room darker than necessary. When they'd sold him the lodge and the cabin he'd grown up in, they'd moved to an older home deep in the woods. He'd never liked the fact that they'd moved to forget the pain of losing his sister, but he'd offered to help remodel the place and brighten it up with nice paint and new furniture.

They'd refused.

Of course, there were no Christmas lights. Not a single holiday decoration. It was as dull as his parents' souls had been since they lost Noelle.

He stayed perched on the edge of the sofa cushion. "I just came to say that I can't do this anymore. I'm sorry. I love you both, but I can't keep tiptoeing around the fact that we lost someone we loved."

His mother's eyes moistened.

His father's usual frown deepened. "Now, son—"

"No." Ross held up a hand. "I have to say this. If you want any kind of relationship with me in the future, I've got to get this out, because it should've been said a long time ago."

A heavy breath filled his lungs, then he pushed it out again. "When Noelle passed, it was like you died with her. You forgot that I still needed you. I was just a teenager, and I needed..." He thought of Kimberly having no real parents at all. "I ... I needed parents, but you weren't there."

He stumbled over his words.

Kimberly had had even less support growing up. He'd promised not to let her down. Promised her that he wasn't going anywhere.

Then foolishly, had done exactly what he'd promised her he'd never do.

He rubbed the corner of his eyes with a thumb and forefinger, then continued. "I lost Noelle, too, but neither of you thought of how I needed to grieve, or what I needed to do so I could move on from her loss." His voice grew ragged, because for the first time, he was admitting to himself that his parents hadn't just been grieving for years. They'd been selfish, too.

He'd been their enabler and had hurt the most important person in his life with harsh words over a sign with his sister's name on it. All to keep enabling his mom and dad.

His mother sniffed.

His father stared at the dark brown shag carpet.

"I got over it. I forgave you guys because I knew what you went through." He let the years of pent-up frustration and anger toward his parents tumble out all at once. "But *you* never got over it. Out of respect for you, I've played along and not mentioned Noelle's name in your presence, but I was wrong. And you were wrong for asking that of me. We should've been talking about her all along, and celebrating her life the way she wanted us to."

"Oh, son." His mom's voice shook. "I had no idea."

"Sure you did, Mom. You knew exactly what you were doing." Ross's tone filled with sorrow. "You wanted her memory to fade so the pain would fade, too." His throat thickened. "But it didn't, did it?" He looked around the dark, dreary room. "It only got worse for you because her memory is always going to live in our hearts, the way it should." He scrubbed a hand down his face. "Tonight, I hurt someone very special who didn't deserve it because I'm so scared to talk about Noelle. I mean really *talk* about her. I never fully explained the situation to Kimberly in detail. How unfair it was to expect her to just *know.*" Like she should be able to read his mind or something. What he was going to say next was going to be hard for all of them. "Noelle would be so disappointed in us."

His mom burst into tears.

His father went to her and rubbed her shoulder. "Ross, I think you should leave now."

"No." His mom shook her head. "He's right about all of it." She reached for the small side table next to her chair and retrieved a tissue. "When your friend, Kimberly, called us, she didn't say what she had planned, but I realized how much of your life we've been missing. How much we must've let slip by unnoticed when you were still a teenager." Mom dabbed at her nose. "I didn't even know you had such a wonderful girlfriend, who obviously loves you, or she wouldn't have gone to so much trouble."

Ross's heart stopped beating.

Kimberly had been doing what she always did—good deeds for others. Never for herself. And he'd broken his promise by walking away from her for it.

Ross stood. "I've got to go." He doubted Kimberly was still his girlfriend. She was too smart to stick with an idiot like him, but he had to go find out for sure.

He had to fight for her the way no one else ever had, because she was worth it.

As he reached the doorway that led into the hall, he turned. "I love you both. You know that, right?"

"Of course, we know, son," his dad said. "We love you, too. You won't be able to comprehend how much we love you until you have kids of your own."

He stared into their blazing fireplace for a moment.

If he ever had kids of own. He'd likely chased off the only person he'd ever cared enough about for their relationship to possibly lead to children.

"I'll see you soon," he promised his parents, then turned to go.

He couldn't get out the front door fast enough. The tires on his old pickup squalled as he backed out of the drive and headed toward Red River city limits.

There was only one way to find out if Kimberly would ever forgive him, and that was to go ask. Talk was cheap to a person who'd lived the kind of life Kimberly had, though.

Maybe he could convince her by showing her. Then maybe, just maybe, she'd give him one more chance, whether he deserved it or not.

CHAPTER FOURTEEN

Kimberly let the firefighters know that she'd be delivering the gifts around the state herself, then she spent the next few days letting the rest of the packages arrive via their mail carrier. When she had every wish accounted for, so not one kid on her list would go without, she packed a bag and planned her delivery route.

On a conference table at her office, she unfolded an old-fashioned road map she'd picked up at the pharmacy. With a sparkly purple pen, she started marking dots on the map. Every time she scribbled a small circle, she checked that name off her list. If she could plan out a route and get on the road by lunchtime, she might even be able to get back to Red River to have Christmas dinner with Angelique and her gigantic extended *Italiano* family, who were arriving in droves.

After she'd flipped through every page on her clipboard and filled the map with purple dots, she grabbed her small bag filled with every color of clothing she could find in her closet, just because she damn well could, and tossed the bag over one shoulder.

"Hey, girlfriend." She blew into Angelique's office. "I'm blowing this pop stand." She put on a pair of fashionable sunglasses from the dollar store. "Maybe I'll be back in time for Christmas dinner at your place."

Angelique looked up from the file she was reading. "Oh. Okay. Well, do what you can."

Kimberly peered over the rim of her shades. "What? No Italian mob threat if I don't show up for turkey and pumpkin pie?" That was new. Angelique loved for Kimberly to stick around for family gatherings. It took the heat off of Angelique when her aunts started in with their *charming* advice. Instead of critiquing her marriage and parenting skills, they focused more on Kimberly's unorthodox wardrobe and hairstyle choices as the cause of her single marital status.

Since that was absolutely the truth, Kimberly didn't mind the well-meaning constructive criticism.

"Sorry," Angelique said. "I'm just trying to finish up this case before all of my family arrives and starts smothering me and the kids. You know how they are."

Kimberly did. And Angelique was lucky to have those nervy overbearing Italian women doting on her.

Angelique gave her a sympathetic smile. "I haven't been very supportive after what's happened with Ross." She tapped the file. "If we didn't have bills to pay, maybe I'd be a better friend."

"To heck with Ross." He hadn't come looking for Kimberly. Hadn't called.

She didn't need support because of him. "He's history."

Emptiness filled the pit of her stomach.

Except that he wasn't history. Not by a long shot.

Eventually, he would be, though.

"I'm over it," Kimberly said.

Angelique gave her a worried look. "You sure about that?"

Now that Red River was completely and uselessly decorated because of two meddling elderly sisters' evil plot to make a love match, Kimberly could get on with helping others. That was all that mattered to her. "So over it."

Angelique frowned and glanced at her watch. "*I'm* not so sure.

Maybe you should sit with me for a while. Have another cup of coffee with me before you hit the road."

Kimberly rolled her eyes. "You're the best friend I could've ever asked for, but stop it. And that obnoxious family of yours are the only people who've ever treated *me* like family, so lay off them and enjoy their visit." Kimberly slid the shades up the bridge of her nose again. "I'll try my best to make it back before they leave Red River so they can complain about my hair and clothes. Maybe I can even pick up a few pairs of obnoxious leggings while I'm gone. That should make up for me missing the first few days of them giving you endless marriage and child-rearing pointers."

"Are you sure you're going to be okay out on the road alone?" Angelique asked. "I'm worried about you."

"Well, don't. Alone is what I need right now." Kimberly should've never stopped being alone. Letting Ross in had been a mistake. "I'll call you every night." She spun on a heel to leave.

"You better!" Angelique yelled after her.

Kimberly trotted down the back stairs. She threw her bag into the passenger seat, then climbed behind the wheel to go make a bunch of wishes come true.

Exactly the thing she was supposed to be doing.

So she'd allowed herself to get distracted by an old woman and her gavel. And by a man who had been too tempting in bed and too slick with words for Kimberly to resist.

Her head was clear, again, and she was back on track.

She turned the key in the ignition.

A sickly whirring sound filled the cab, then died out completely.

She tried to fire up the engine again.

That time it didn't even whir.

No. *No, no, no!*

This could not be happening.

She got out and kicked the tire. Screamed into the air.

Kimberly didn't bother going back into the office to ask Angelique for help. Ang was an incredible attorney, but she had zero skills with automobiles. Instead, Kimberly started out on foot, going to every business, every restaurant and café. She went up and down Main Street asking anyone and everyone for help. No one could.

No one *would*.

The universe hated her. Or maybe it was just the people of Red River who hated her.

Everyone in town suggested she call the only mechanic in Red River—Ross Armstrong.

Hell no.

She traipsed back to her office. Hours had gone by and it was getting dark. Angelique must've gone home because her car was gone from the parking lot behind their office. Only the broken-down moving truck was left, parked diagonal across several spaces. Kimberly folded her arms on top of the hood and buried her face in them.

What was wrong with these people? Why on earth had she uprooted her life and moved to a place that couldn't lend a helping hand to someone who needed it?

Even if she could find someone to tow the truck to a nearby town for repairs, she'd never be able to deliver all the gifts before Christmas. She turned and slid down to the ground, leaning back against the grill of the truck.

As she put her head in her hands, the sound of a massive automobile engine roared past her office building, obviously traveling down Main Street. Then another. And another, and another.

She wasn't going to get up and walk around to the front of her building to see what was going on because she didn't care. She was tired of Red River.

She was tired, period.

After the holidays, she'd break the news to her bestie that this town wasn't for her, then she'd move her practice back to Taos, where she could actually make a difference in the community.

She looked up at the sky, the purple hue slowly darkening to black. "When am I ever going to catch a break in this life?" She wasn't sure who she was asking. God, the universe in general. Hell, if Santa was up there somewhere loading up his sleigh, maybe he'd hear her plea.

"Kimberly?" A head, belonging to Cal Wells appeared from around the side of the truck. When he saw her sitting there, he stepped to the front. "Ms. Clydelle sent me to find you."

Kimberly was no longer going to be at the beck and call of the old woman's gavel. "Tell Madam Chairperson I'm unavailable, Sweet Cheeks."

"Um ... okay, but..." Even in the dark, Kimberly could hear the blush in Cal's voice.

So she poured it on even more. "You don't mind me calling you Sweet Cheeks, do you?" Why not? It was her last hoorah in that town.

Cal cleared his throat. "There's something going on in the park. Ms. Clydelle said you needed to come quick."

Kimberly grumbled with extra flare just so the universe ... and Cal, AKA Sweet Cheeks, would know how fed up she was.

"Fine." She pushed herself to stand. "But this is the last time that woman, or anyone else in this town, tells me what to do." She followed Cal to his truck and climbed into the passenger seat.

He pulled around to Main Street and turned right in the direction of the park. As it came into view, Kimberly leaned forward, letting her eyes bug out. "What in the world?" Her head swiveled toward Sweet Cheeks.

His expression said he was a little scared of her. "Don't know." Both of his shoulders lifted. "All I know is I'm supposed to deliver you to the park, where Ms. Clydelle is waiting."

A line of luxury tour buses sat along the curb in front of the park, one in front of the other.

Cal slowed, but before he could come to a complete stop, Kimberly had the door open and she hit the pavement at a dead run. When she rounded the bus, she froze.

Kids of all ages were filing out of the buses, and dozens of Red River business owners—the same business owners who'd turned her down when she needed help repairing the moving truck—were directing the kids over to the Wishing Tree.

Chairperson Clydelle and her sister-in-crime, Ms. Francine, both shuffled over to her.

"Nice of you to show up, dear," Ms. Clydelle said. "It wouldn't have been right to have the kids open gifts without you, since you're the one who made all this happen."

No, she'd failed to make it happen. "How...?" Her hands went to her cheeks. "Who...?" She couldn't decide what question to ask first. "The gifts are at my office."

Ms. Francine shook her head and pointed down the street, her purse swinging on her arm. "No, they're not. They're right here."

Kimberly followed Ms. Francine's boney pointing finger. The moving truck that had been broken down behind her office was slowly moving toward them. It eased into a spot behind the last bus.

Cal and a group of his firefighter buddies formed an assembly line starting at the tree and stretching all the way to the curb next to the truck. Kimberly craned her neck to see who was driving as the door opened ... and Ross stepped out from behind the wheel.

She held her breath.

Ross went around to the back of the truck, and the human assembly line started rolling toward the tree, with the firefighters handing off packages one after the other.

Ross strolled in her direction.

When her lungs nearly burst, she remembered to breathe again.

He stopped several feet away. "Evening, ladies," he said to Ms. Clydelle and Ms. Francine. "Thanks for your help."

"You're very welcome." Ms. Clydelle looked extremely pleased with herself.

Ms. Francine clucked her tongue. "It would've been a shame not to finish what we started."

"You've all been conspiring on this?" Kimberly's hands went to her hips. "Behind my back?"

Ross shrugged as if to say *I'm so busted.* "I had to keep you in Red River somehow. These fine ladies were good enough to send out word that no one in town was to help fix the truck."

"Wait..." Kimberly glared at the two sisters, who didn't seem the least bit remorseful, then back at Ross.

He shrugged again. "I loosened the distributor cap on the truck." He smiled and lifted a finger. "Mechanic, remember? Thank goodness you left the keys in it, or I would've had to hot wire it."

She rolled her eyes and threw both hands in the air. "I've been going out of my mind trying to figure out how to get the gifts to the kids before Christmas."

"Sorry to put you through more..." His eyes softened with regret, and he didn't finish the sentence. "It was the only way to keep you from leaving town with the gifts. It's a few days sooner than we'd originally planned, but I hope you don't mind giving out the presents a little early. It was the only way I could make it all come together here in Red River before you took off in that truck like Santa Claus on wheels."

Kimberly ran both sets of fingers through her hair. "But how did you know where the kids lived?"

"I asked Angelique to make a copy of the list from your clipboard when you weren't around," cooed Ms. Francine.

"My law partner was in on this, too?" Kimberly gasped.

"Sure was." Angelique walked up behind her and joined their circle. "I was so afraid I wouldn't be able to stall you long enough this morning for Ross to sabotage the truck." She pointed across the park to the bus at the front of the line. "My family came into town a few days early to help out with the chaperoning, food, and whatever else the kids need." She lifted a brow. "All of them. Aunts, uncles, cousins. Even a few I don't recognize. I think they're just pretending to be relatives to feast on my mom's and her sisters' Italian cooking."

Kimberly went up on tippy toes, and sure enough. A few dozen people—all with olive complexions and waving arms in the air like a scene straight out of Moonstruck—were organizing kids on the other side of the park.

"Dear Lord. It's like I've died and gone to Sicily," Kimberly mumbled, then gave her bestie a playful slug. "Thanks, hon. I adore you, ya know."

"I know." Angelique winked. "I better go help out before my grandmother starts teaching the kids how to swear in Italian." She strolled away.

"But where will the kids stay?" Kimberly's mind started spinning. "How can we feed this many people?"

"Every bed and breakfast, hotel, and lodge has dedicated the next few days to these kids," Ross said.

"Cotton Eyed Joe's is providing lunches and Rocket Pizza is providing dinner," Ms. Clydelle added. "Everything's taken care of, so no need to worry."

"I..." Kimberly's voice cracked, and she fought off a prickle behind her eyes. "I don't know what to say."

"Well," Ms. Francine said innocently. "You could say that you forgive poor Ross, here." She swung her purse in his direction. "He's worked hard to make sure this came together so it would be special for you."

She turned her gaze on him and their eyes hooked into each other.

"Ladies," he said to the two sisters without looking away from Kimberly. "Would you mind giving us a minute?"

They waddled off, harrumphing as they went.

"You did all this for me?" she asked, her voice a tangle of emotions.

Ross eased another step closer. "For the kids, too, but mostly for you."

"And the whole town was in on it?" she whispered.

He nodded and took another step. "Pretty much."

"How did you find the buses?" she asked.

"Let's just say I'll be providing free lifetime repairs to my client who owns the buses, and he has a *lot* of expensive classic cars."

Ross scratched his jaw. "I may have also thrown in my classic pickup."

Kimberly let a gasp slip through her lips. "You adore that truck. You rebuilt it yourself. Ross, why?" For a hardass who'd made it her life's mission growing up to never cry in front of anyone, she'd turned pretty soft lately. Tears swam in her eyes. She'd already made up her mind that she was done with Red River. Why'd he have to go and be so sweet?

He took yet another step. "Because I gave you my word. Because of all the people in the world, you're the last one I'd want to let down."

That's all it took for the dam of emotions she'd kept bottled up for so long to break, and tears flowed down her cheeks.

He came up in front of her, framing her face with both of his hands. "Because I love you." He pressed a soft kiss to her lips. "I've loved you for a long time, and the way I blew it by walking away from you when you tried to do something so wonderful for me was inexcusable. I'm so, so sorry."

She covered his hands with hers. "I don't know, Ross." She tried to sniff back the tears, but there was no stopping them. "You did the one thing I don't think I can get past."

"I know." He kissed her forehead. "I'll do whatever it takes to earn your trust again, if you'll give me another chance." He rested his forehead against hers. "But if you don't want me anymore, I'll understand." He chuckled. "I won't like it one damn bit, but I'll respect your decision."

Good Lord.

She wanted to throw herself into his arms and forget every bad thing that had happened. Every hang-up that caused her not to want to open her heart to the man she loved.

But he'd walked away just because she'd made a mistake.

And he was apologizing and asking her to forgive him, like no one else ever had. He'd spent days planning this massive show of affection.

She held on tight, not wanting to let go. Not wanting to lose the safety and security she felt in his arms.

If she pushed him away again, maybe she really was letting herself be a victim of her past. Even good people made mistakes. Mistakes that could be forgiven. Right?

Or was she trying to convince herself that Ross was someone she should count on? The same way she'd tried to convince herself that her parents would come for her, but never did. The same way she'd told herself each foster home would be different, but never was.

If the universe didn't seem to hate her so much, she'd wish for a sign. A sign that would guide her and tell her what to do.

Something tugged at her coat.

She and Ross broke apart and both looked down.

Little Noelle was standing there. "Do you think Santa will make my wish come true?" she asked in the smallest, sweetest voice.

Kimberly glanced at Ross, then they both crouched to Noelle's level to look her in the eye.

"Well, we'll have to see what's in the presents when we open them." Kimberly tweaked Noelle's nose.

Her lip stuck out. "No, I mean my other wish."

Ross gave Kimberly a sympathetic look.

"Sweetie," Ross said. "What other wish?"

Good question. Kimberly didn't remember seeing extra wishes come in from Noelle's foster mom. Hopefully, the one thing Kimberly had wanted to shield these kids from wouldn't happen for little Noelle—disappointment.

"I wished for a mommy and daddy," Noelle said.

"Well, I'm sure wonderful people will come along and want to be your parents," Ross said.

Kimberly drew in a sharp breath and gave her head a quick shake so Ross would stop. He obviously thought it was a kind thing to say. He had no way of knowing that she'd heard it a thousand times growing up, and it hurt more and more every year when it failed to happen. Until she'd finally stopped hoping.

"But they're already here," Noelle said, as though Kimberly and Ross didn't understand.

They didn't, actually. "What do you mean, hon?" Kimberly asked.

Noelle pointed to Ross, then to Kimberly. "I wished for you to be my mommy and daddy."

Kimberly's eyes flew wide.

Ross's mouth turned up and he gave her a hopeful look. "That's the best wish I've ever heard."

Kimberly's heart grew so big at that moment, there was no way she couldn't have let Ross back into it. The possibility of having him in her life and a beautiful little girl named Noelle seemed like more than a Christmas wish come true.

It seemed like a miracle.

EPILOGUE

One year later.

Ross's chest expanded as he stood under the gazebo in the park. A few feet away, *Noelle's Wishing Tree* was lit even brighter, and loaded with even more wishes than there had been the year before.

All of Red River and the kids who'd been brought in to open their gifts looked on, but the most special wedding guests of all were Ross's parents. They were dressed in Christmas colors and both had watery eyes as they stared at Ross and the beautiful little flower girl holding his hand.

The love of his life walked toward him, following a trail that he'd plowed into the snow earlier that day so she wouldn't get the train of her dress wet. She'd borrowed a wedding gown, because Kimberly had been too frugal to waste money on a new dress of her own.

Instead of spending money on a lavish wedding, she'd claimed Red River's park, in it's Christmas winter glory, would be a magnificent backdrop.

She'd been right.

He glanced down at their flower girl, who had scattered a trail of red and green petals along the plowed trail. Noelle *was* wearing a pretty new Christmas dress because Kimberly said nothing was too good for their little girl.

The adoption wasn't finalized yet, but it would be soon.

Noelle rested her hand on Comet's neck, and the dog leaned into her, the blingy antlers Kimberly had made for him wobbled. He'd grown to be Noelle's fierce protector.

But not as fierce as Ross, because he was already certain he'd never let his little girl get married. Or date. Or look at a boy.

He refocused on his bride, and in typical Kimberly fashion, she charged up to the makeshift altar, and whispered, "Hey, big guy. Ready to spend the rest of your life with a misfit?"

"Yep," he whispered back. "Love the hair." She'd been growing it longer, and the silky locks brushed her shoulders.

She blushed. "Thanks." She glanced down at Noelle, then leaned in closer to his ear. "I thought maybe you could wrap it in your hands when we're..." She waggled both brows.

"If that's what the lady wants, that's what the lady will get." He waggled his brows right back at her.

"Another wish fulfilled." She fist-pumped the air. "I'm so damn good at this wish thing."

Deacon West, who'd been ordained and become Pastor West since last Christmas, stepped up in front of them and began to explain why they were all gathered.

It was all a blur. Ross couldn't keep his eyes or his thoughts off Kimberly. And really, he fully understood why they were gathered. It was to witness the happiest day in his life, in the greatest town on earth, with the best people in the world looking on as witnesses.

And now, he, Kimberly, Noelle, Comet, and any other little Armstrongs who might come along would be part of Red River as a family.

In Ross's book, that was proof enough that wishes really did come true.

———

I want to offer a personal heartfelt THANK YOU to my readers for following this series from start to finish. It was my first published series, and I have mixed emotions now that's it's over. I'm going to miss it, but I'm excited to delve into new projects set in utterly romantic locations with incredibly sexy characters.

Rest assured, all of the wonderful quirky characters who make up the soul of Red River will live on my my heart. I hope they will live on in yours, too.

———

Need to catch up on the rest of the series? One-Click IT'S IN HIS HEART and see where it all began!

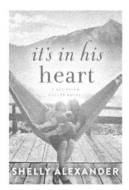

Reviews are an author's best friend! They spread the word to others who enjoy the same books as you. So be sure to leave a review for IT'S IN HIS CHRISTMAS WISH on AMAZON, B&N, GOODREADS, BOOKBUB and any other favorite sites.

And don't miss my DARE ME series! Set on the picturesque vacation island of Angel Fire Falls, it's a sizzling series about secrets and second chances.

One-Click DARE ME ONCE!

Sin up for my VIPeep Reader List to find out about new books, awesome giveaways, and exclusive content including excerpts and deleted scenes: SHELLY'S VIPEEP READER LIST

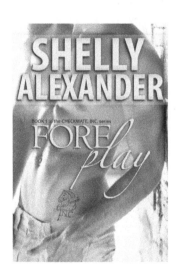

Do you like more steam in your romance novels? Try my super sizzling series of erotic rom coms. Download FOREPLAY now.

About the Checkmate Inc. Series:

· · ·

Leo Foxx, Sex Moore, and Oz Strong spent their youths studying a chessboard, textbooks...and women from afar. Now they're players in the city that never sleeps. Gone are their shy demeanors, replaced with muscle, style, and enough sex appeal to charm women of all ages, shapes, and cup sizes. They've got it all, including a multimillion-dollar business called Checkmate Inc.—a company they founded right out of college.

Some guys are late bloomers, but once they hit their stride, they make up for lost time.

And the bonus? The founding partners of Checkmate Inc. didn't become successful and smokin' hot by accident. They were smart enough to surround themselves with guys who helped them transform into the men they are today. So get ready for more stories about the hotties who are connected to Checkmate Inc.

A fun, flirty, and dirty contemporary series of STAND-ALONES in which the sizzling hot players of Checkmate Inc. and the guys who helped them get to where they are all meet their matches.

MORE TITLES BY SHELLY:

Shelly's titles with a little less steam (still sexy, though!):

The Red River Valley Series

It's In His Heart – Coop & Ella's Story

It's In His Touch – Blake & Angelique's Story

It's In His Smile – Talmadge & Miranda's Story

It's In His Arms – Mitchell & Lorenda's Story

It's In His Forever - Langston & His Secret Love's Story

It's In His Song - Dylan & Hailey's Story

It's In His Christmas Wish - Ross & Kimberly's Story

The Angel Fire Falls Series

Dare Me Once — Trace & Lily's Story

Dare Me Again — Elliott & Rebel's Story

Dare Me Now - TBA

Dare Me Always - TBA

Shelly's sizzling titles (with a lot of steam):

The Checkmate Inc. Series

ForePlay – Leo & Chloe's Story

Rookie Moves – Dex & Ava's Story

Get Wilde – Ethan & Adeline's Story

Sinful Games – Oz & Kendall's Story

Wilde Rush - Jacob & Grace's Story TBA

ABOUT THE AUTHOR

Shelly Alexander is the author of contemporary romances that are sometimes sweet, sometimes sizzling, and always sassy. A 2014 Golden Heart® finalist, and a 2019 RITA® finalist, and a 2019 HOLT Medallion finalist, she grew up traveling the world, earned a bachelor's degree in marketing, and worked in the business world for twenty-five years. With four older brothers, she and her older sister watched every *Star Trek* episode ever made, joined the softball team instead of ballet class, and played with G.I. Joes while the Barbie Corvette stayed tucked in her closet. When she had three sons of her own, she decided to escape her male-dominated world by reading romance novels and has been hooked ever since. Now she spends her days writing steamy contemporary romances while tending to two spoiled toy poodles named Mozart and Midge. And she grew up to own her very own Corvette, so Barbie can keep hers.

Be the first to know about Shelly's new releases, giveaways, appearances, and bonus scenes not included in her books! Sign up for her Reader List and receive VIP treatment:
shellyalexander.net

Other ways to stalk Shelly:
BookBub
Amazon
Email

Cover design by **Erin Dameron Hill**

Editing by **Alicia Carmical**

Print edition ISBN: 978-1-7341498-0-7

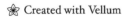 Created with Vellum

CPSIA information can be obtained
at www.ICGtesting.com
Printed in the USA
LVHW032309061219
639739LV00003B/336/P